The Faery Road

C.J. McCarthy

Come away, O human child!
To the waters and the wild
With a faery, hand in hand,

For the world's more full of weeping than you can understand.

\- W.B. Yeats
The Stolen Child

'You know that old gate was open on my way back today?'

Daniel frowned at the bowl of vegetable stir-fry Keira handed him, then at the question. 'Which gate is this?'

'The one by the forest there,' Keira said as she sat next to him with her own. She was trying to eat less meat, thereby saving the planet somehow, which meant Daniel had to eat less meat too. 'Usually tied off with a rope.' Then, regarding the food. 'What do you think?'

'Oh you mean the faery gate.' Daniel bit into the stir-fry. 'It's good, yeah.'

Keira snorted. 'The what?'

'The faery gate. Forest people, you know. The fair folk.'

'What? That gate there? You're making this up.'

'Am not,' Daniel said through a mouthful of chickpeas. 'Here be faeries.'

'Says who?'

'Says Marie, the Lord rest her soul.'

'Your grandmother?'

'The one and only.'

Keira paused. 'I thought you said she was crazy.'

'Oh, totally bonkers, but that doesn't mean she couldn't tell a good story. In fact I'd argue the opposite.'

'So she told you about these faeries then?'

'That she did, along with a whole rake of other things that I'm sure I'm still bearing the emotional scars of to this day.'

'Well, what did she say?'

Daniel rolled his eyes. 'Can't this wait?' He pointed at the television. 'You're missing the best part.' On the screen, Billy Bob Thornton was about to shoot up the headquarters of an organised crime syndicate.

Keira picked up the remote and paused the tv. 'No, tell me now. What's behind the gate?'

'Ugh. It's just an old famine road.'

This, it seemed, was the last thing he should have said. Keira's eyes lit up.

'No way, seriously? That's what I did my history project on in Leaving Cert.' She leaned forward. 'Did you know that some historians theorise that there are people buried underneath the roads? That they dropped dead of exhaustion and the British officers ordered the workers to just build over them? Gruesome stuff.'

'What did you read that in, the 'RA Weekly?'

'It's the 'RA *Seachtaine,* thank you very much.'

'Oh shut up.'

'You shut up.'

'Alright, I will,' Daniel said. He hit *play* and the scene resumed.

Keira paused it again. Daniel looked at her.

'Show me,' she said.

Daniel rolled his eyes again. 'It's half-five, Keira.'

'You keep doing that and they'll fall out of your skull.'

'We'll go tomorrow. I've to get those chapters off to Theo, remember?'

'You will, yeah.' Keira rose to get her coat. 'Come on, it doesn't get dark till eleven anyways.'

'Jesus Christ, can't a man have his dinner in peace?'

Keira folded her arms. 'Finish it and we'll go.'

'For god's... Aren't you scared of the faeries at all? My great-great-grandfather barely got out of those woods with his life you know.'

'Oh shut up and eat your food.'

Daniel looked down at his vegetable stir-fry and grimaced. 'I'm actually not that hungry.'

*

The gate was open as Keira had said it would be. The frayed rope hung limply from the tree branch it had been tied to since before Daniel was born. After years of storm and weathering, the knot had finally come undone.

'So basically, to hear her tell it, the British captain in charge of the work schemes around here decided that building a useless road to nowhere would be too good for the scum-of-the-earth, starving Irish.'

'Naturally.'

'And this captain, Officer Lancey I think his name was, figured what better way to build spirit and boost morale than to have them cut into the forest here and build a road through to other end. That way, they wouldn't just get to split up and set down massive stone after massive stone, but they had the added luxury of getting to chop down every tree in their path as well.'

'Jesus. Sounds like a typical Brit alright.'

Daniel grinned. 'You sound just like her.' He could even picture his granny's wrinkled face now, hunched over in her shawl as she rocked back and forth in her chair before the fire, scaring him senseless. 'Anyways, when the locals saw where he meant to build this road, they begged Lancey not to go through with it. *You'll damn us all, the sky will collapse,* that sort of thing.'

'I take it he didn't listen.'

'That he did not. No mention of faeries or faery forts could convince Lancey that the lazy Irish were being anything other than lazy Irish, so even when they downed tools right in front of him, he just shrugged and told them they'd be back once their stomachs bid them.'

Keira looked around and down the empty road, which stretched into the wooded horizon ahead. 'Seems he was right.'

'About that, yeah. About other things, not so much. Three weeks they chopped and built, built and chopped, taking their handful of maize or corn or whatever the fuck it was in the evenings, but on the afternoon that would have seen the start of the fourth week of building, something happened.'

'How terribly exciting.'

'It is, actually.' Stones crunched under Daniel's feet as he shut the gate behind them, and, taken by some perverse instinct, re-did the knot at its end.

Keira watched him do it with a coy smile. 'Is that so the faeries don't get out?'

'Obviously,' Daniel said, pointing the way forward. 'As you can see for yourself, the workers made some decent progress, but they still hadn't reached the faery fort. Another day or two, though, and they'd be right on top of it. The faeries couldn't allow that.'

'Oh they wouldn't, would they?'

Daniel shook his head. 'Never in a million years would they allow such blasphemy, but they're tricksy bastards, faeries are, and they knew better than to reveal themselves to the workers.'

'Of course, of course, they'd never dream of something so gauche,' Keira said, turning to smile at him in speckled-light glow.

'Quite,' Daniel agreed. 'What they did do, mind you, was they started to whisper.'

'Oh wow.'

'Wow indeed. Ever so soft and gentle, they whispered, but each man heard it as if it were coming right from within the centre of his skull. Even Officer Lancey heard it, and that kicked him off his perch, not that he'd be the kind to admit it. The workers all looked around, terrified, not knowing what to do, no idea where the noise was coming from, but Lancey just yelled at them. Keep cutting, keep breaking rocks, there'd be fifty lashes for the first man to stop. But all the while the whispering continued –'

'How ominous.'

'– and even as the men went to chop, they suddenly found that they couldn't anymore. Their metal tools and wooden hafts had turned to vine and leaves in their hands. The faeries had had enough destruction of their property, it was time to return the favour.'

'Big on drama these faeries, aren't they?'

'Oh big time, but they weren't done yet. You see to them, the trees were living, breathing creatures, just like you or me, and they saw what the workers had done, chopping them all down to build a useless road over their corpse, well they saw it as murder. And so they sought to repay that too, only they were very clever about it.'

'They do sound frightfully clever, waiting for the last possible minute to act and all.'

Daniel waved her away. 'Once a faery starts speaking, they have a way of making the listener fall into a sort of trance, where they don't really know what they're doing. They do this by telling them everything they want to hear, and in doing so, they lull the listener into a false sense of security. That's where we as humans are at our most vulnerable, and the faeries at their most despicable.

'They told the workers to line up along both sides of the road they'd built, Officer Lancey included, and if they all did so in perfect order, from beginning to end, not only would they escape punishment, they'd be rewarded for their efforts. Even if the workers didn't believe them – though I have no doubt that they did, faeries are very persuasive – the trance they'd been placed under would have seen them follow their instructions just the same.

6

'So each man among them lined up along the newly built famine road and, between them all, they just about stretched from end to end, with one left over. That one, according to good old Marie, was my great-great-grandfather. The faeries made him watch as they warped the flesh and cracked the skin of every last one of his friends, family, and finagling British bastards. He stood there helpless as they choked and spluttered and gagged, no air getting in, no air coming out, unable to move a muscle as their skin turned to bark and their blood turned to sap, their hair to grass and their veins to vines. When he tried to look away, a pair of hands as cold as ice grasped a hold of him from behind and forced his eyes open, forced him to see all that he would not, and burned it into his memory forever.'

'Pretty grim,' Keira said, and rapped her knuckles against the bark of a tree. 'I suppose this is one of the unlucky souls, then?'

Daniel nodded, spread his arms to encapsulate the whole of their surroundings. 'All around you, nothing but unlucky souls.' He winked. 'Except for me. My great-great-grandfather was the only one of them to be spared, and because of that, here we are today.'

'Always one left to tell the tale,' Keira muttered. Then she frowned. 'How come they killed them all? Why not just kill the officer, this Lancey?'

Daniel shrugged. 'Faeries gonna faery, Keira, what do you want me to say?' He grabbed her arm and leaned forward. In imitation of his best Granny Cawley voice, he wagged a finger at her. '*If the faeries really cared about justice, or protecting their*

7

sanctum, they would have done away with your great-great-grandfather too, and left us all none the wiser. But they didn't do that, because they don't care about justice at all. All they care about are their little games, and getting one over on us lowly human folk.'

Keira gave him a sidelong look and shrugged off his grip. 'Charming.' She pursed her lips. 'And you say she told you all this the day after your parents died?'

'The first time yeah,' Daniel said. 'I'd tried to run off because I didn't want to live with her and hid out here for an hour or two. When she finally got a hold of me, she told me that story and I've stayed fairly well clear of the place since.'

'I'm not surprised,' Keira said. 'I can't imagine what it was like growing up in that house.'

'It wasn't so bad. You get used to it.'

The only child of two only children, Daniel was something of an anomaly in Ireland. Growing up, he didn't have any cousins or aunties or uncles, and after his parents' death it was just him and Granny Cawley most of the time, except when Joe came over to visit. If he hadn't gotten used to it, God knew where he'd be.

As the gate shrunk into the distance behind them, Keira turned to face Daniel. 'How far does it go, anyways?'

'I'm not really sure, maybe a kilometre or so that-a-way.' It was quite the sight to behold, the endless road through the woods, with the trees running in parallel lines alongside until the eye lost focus.

'And then it just stops dead?'

8

'Yeah, and the forest starts up again then,' Daniel said. 'There's supposed to be a clearing somewhere past the trees though, if you care to venture that far.'

'Would that be where one might find the faery fort?'

'So the locals claim.'

'And what do you claim, local as you are?'

Daniel shrugged. 'I'd have to see it first.'

'Hmm,' Keira said. 'We'll see how we're feeling once we get to the end. That stir-fry isn't sitting right with me.'

'Maybe that's because three-hundred calories isn't enough for dinner.'

'Shut up, you didn't even eat yours.'

'Can you blame me?'

'Ugh.' Keira shook her head and took off down the road.

'Alright, alright, wait up,' Daniel called, and chased after her.

The sun had trouble penetrating the forest trees, so the famine road was bathed predominantly in shadow, with little flecks of sparkling light illuminating patches of stone, casting them an almost golden hue.

'The trees really are incredible,' Keira said, 'what are they, do you know?'

'Besides all the worldly remains of countless famine workers, you mean? Alder, I think. Though I never went to Scouts so don't hold me to that.'

'No, I think you're right. It is amazing the way they line up one after another like that. I can see where the stories come from.'

'It's something alright,' Daniel said. Looking at all the perfect uniformity that surrounded him, he couldn't help but see where the stories came from too. A cold shiver ran down his spine, and he chided himself for being childish. His granny sure knew how to tell them. Probably where he got it from.

They walked on in silence for some distance, letting the quiet sounds of the forest guide their way. Even as they did so, Daniel got the uneasy sense, deep in the pit of his shoulders, that they were being watched. Ridiculous, of course, but he was about to say it to Keira, see if she'd felt it too, when she spoke.

'Oh,' Keira said, and stopped. They were a good five or six-hundred metres along the road, and the old gate was now the size of a fingernail behind them. 'Is there a story behind this one?'

Daniel stepped over to the tree she'd pointed at, dismissing thoughts of voyeurs from his mind. It was Alder like the rest, but with a significant scarring in its bark at about hip-length, like someone or something had tried to take a big whack out of it.

'Maybe someone tried to cut it down?'

Keira shook her head. 'It looks more like a dent than someone going at it with an axe.'

'Weird,' Daniel said. 'Unfortunately I've no story for it though. Come on, let's keep going, we're almost at the end.'

'Alright,' Keira said, but she looked back at the damaged tree for a moment longer before finally turning away.

'Do you think there's any bodies buried under this road?' she asked, now that the gate and civilisation had disappeared behind them.

'Jesus Christ, Keira, will you relax?'

'Apart from the ones that live in the trees I mean.'

'Stop.'

'I mean it's possible that they're buried underground, and the tree roots feed off them. That would mean they're alive in the trees, I suppose. Did you ever hear that story about the man who killed his wife and buried her in his garden? The only reason they found her was because the police dogs smelled her scent coming out of the tree's branches. Apparently the roots had dug their way through her corpse, and were feeding off –'

'For the love of God, will you stop!' Daniel snapped, far harsher than he'd meant to.

'Sorr-ry,' Keira said, unfazed. 'What's got your knickers in a twist?'

'Nothing,' Daniel said, but the deepening knot in his shoulders said otherwise. 'I don't know, maybe you just shouldn't be saying those things around here.'

'Aw, is the poor boy frightened of the big scary faeries?' Keira teased. 'What a poor boy.'

'Shut up,' Daniel said. That knot wasn't going anywhere, and he glanced back the way they'd come to make sure they were truly alone.

'Look, there's the end,' Keira pointed, and Daniel's head whipped back round to see that she was right.

The two set their feet down where the stone of man-made road ended and the forest grass and trees took up again. At this point, the trees no longer stood side by side, one after the other, in perfect rows, but rather had vast gaps interspersed between them, a return to the wild.

'Wow,' Keira said, 'so this is where the forest really begins.'

'More where it resumes,' Daniel said, looking deep into the trees. 'It began back at the gate.'

'Don't be such a smart arse.'

'I wasn't,' Daniel said, and turned to her. She was standing in one of the few bright spots where the sunlight permeated the woods, and her face shone radiantly up at him. 'There was something about this place that I can't remember. When I hid out here that time. God I must have been, what, five?'

'About which?' Keira asked. 'The road?'

'No, the end of it. This place right here.' He looked around. 'Something about one of the trees. I think one was different?'

Both he and Keira turned their heads to study the trees that lined the road up to its end. 'They all look the same to me,' Keira said. 'All Alder, Mr. Scout Leader, sir.'

Daniel agreed, but couldn't shake the feeling that something was off, something was different, something was missing. Or something wasn't. His eyes widened.

'What, what is it?' Keira asked.

Daniel didn't pay her any attention. He marched over to his right, and began inspecting the trees on that side of the road, starting at the very end and working his way down.

Keira followed after him. 'What are you doing?'

He got to four trees down and stopped. He looked at the third one and the fifth one, before rubbing his hand along the bark of the tree in the middle, the fourth. He backed away slowly, and when he turned back to Keira, he smiled.

'This tree,' he said, and pointed at the culprit, 'didn't used to be here. I remember now.' Daniel recalled that summers day so long ago, the day after his parents' crash. 'There was a gap between these two, and a little sapling, right here.'

'So you're saying that there used to be a tree-sprout here, and now there's a tree.' Keira patted him on the shoulder. 'Fascinating stuff Daniel, really. I think all this fresh air is getting to your head. You need to get out more, you're spending too much time cooped up in that study of yours.'

Still cruising off the high of remembrance, Daniel's smile took on a different tone. 'Maybe you're right,' he said. 'But I'll tell you one thing is for sure, the two of us don't get outside together anywhere near enough.'

'What are you getting at, mister?'

'Oh I don't know,' Daniel said, and laid a finger on her hair, shining in the light. The discovery of the "missing" tree had been such a rush, it had whisked away those niggling tendrils of unease. There were no thoughts of watching eyes on him now, and even if there had been, he wouldn't have cared. 'What do you say we take a run through these trees, see if we can't find somewhere more secluded?'

Keira raised her eyebrows and looked around. Not an artificial sound creeped in from any direction, their only companion the faint rustling of wind against the trees. 'I'd say here is plenty secluded.'

'Oh really?' Daniel asked, stepping close to her.

'Oh yeah,' Keira said, stepping close to him.

'Well come here then,' Daniel said.

And she did.

22

Daniel barely had time to put the car keys in the bowl before Keira burst into the hallway, still in her pyjamas.

'Well, how did it go?'

Daniel shrugged. 'Alright, yeah,' he said, and hid his grin as he shuffled past her into the kitchen.

'What does "alright, yeah" mean?' Keira asked, hot on his tail. 'Did you get it or not? You got it, didn't you? Please tell me you got it.'

Daniel grabbed a carton of milk from the fridge and drank it straight from the bottle. Wiping away his milk-stache, he tilted his head. 'We came to an agreement.'

Keira snatched the carton from him. 'You're disgusting. What sort of agreement?'

'The full shebang.'

Keira's mouth fell open. 'Really?'

Daniel nodded, and smiled at last, ear to ear. 'Really.'

The full shebang equated to ten thousand euros, directly deposited into Daniel's bank account courtesy of Theo White and the Nu-Wave publishing company, for the rights to his second novel. It was a far-cry more than he'd seen for the first, and for a stay-at-home writer and his student-teacher girlfriend, it was substantial.

'Woohoo!' Keira cried as she wrapped Daniel in a hug and showered him with kisses. When at last she pulled back, he felt even more light-headed than before. Life was his dream and everyone else just happened to be living in it.

'Let's do something to celebrate,' Keira said.

'There's a crate of Bud in the shed.'

Keira scrunched up her face at him. 'Not that you big hermit, let's get out of the house. The fair's on in town, you know?'

Daniel did know. In fact, the slim bulge in his coat pocket meant he had great reason to know. 'Believe it or not, I was going to suggest that myself.'

'Wow, look at you. Trying to get out of the house before you're all rich and famous is it?'

'I'm already rich.'

'Come on then,' Keira said, and grabbed his hand. 'You can spoil me.' But rather than the front door, she led him to the bedroom.

'I thought we were going to the fair?'

'We are,' Keira said, 'but first you have to get me out of these pyjamas.'

Daniel grinned. 'Now that I can do.'

*

'Oh, let's try this one,' Keira said, stopping in front of a water pistol stand with rows of packaged goldfish on the shelves behind.

'Three euro to play,' the greasy teenager behind the stand said, and gestured lamely at the stack of pins behind him. 'Knock'em all down and you get a fish.'

Daniel gave Keira a quizzical look. 'Why do you want a goldfish?'

'Because look how sad they are in their little plastic bags' Keira said. 'They need a real home, or at least a bowl with a fake fish-castle or something.'

Daniel watched the fish swim back and forth within their tiny plastic confines and wondered how a fish-castle differentiated from a castle-castle. In any case, they did look pretty sad. 'Can't these things grow to the size of your forearm?'

The teenager shrugged. 'Ask for the money and hand them the pistol, that's all they told me.'

'I don't know…' Daniel said. He'd never had a pet before, he wouldn't know what to do with it.

'Oh you big coward,' Keira said. 'Here.' She reached into her purse and handed the teenager a fiver. In return, she received a water pistol and her change.

'You get three squirts.'

Daniel narrowed his eyes at the suspect choice of words, but Keira either didn't notice or didn't care.

There were six metal pins, each about the size of a forefinger, stacked in a triangle, three at the bottom, two in the middle and one on top. Keira eyed them carefully, then said out of the side of her mouth to Daniel: 'Watch how it's done.'

Her first "squirt" hit right where the middle two met, and knocked the both of them, as well as the one on top, clean off. The bottom-left pin wobbled for a moment, but settled, leaving three still standing. Sensing a weakness there, Keira ignored the wobbly pin and aimed instead for the bottom right, which she knocked off instantly. The bottom-middle and left pins remained, a slight gap between them.

'Here's the tricky part,' Keira said. She looked down the water-gun's fictional sight and closed her left eye. With her right forefinger, she pulled the trigger and her final squirt flew. It hit the middle pin straight down the centre and knocked it over, missing the left pin, but as the one she'd hit fell, the force of its rumble against the wood caused the remaining wobbly pin to collapse.

Keira's eyes danced. 'Does that count?'

'Sure,' the teenager said. 'I don't care.'

'Woohoo,' she cheered, and turned and hugged Daniel. 'I won!'

'I saw,' Daniel said. The game wasn't rigged, at least. He wondered what the actual market value of the goldfish were if the people running this stand were able to sell them for as little as three euro a head.

'Which one do you want?' the teenager asked.

'I don't know,' Keira said. 'I want them all. Daniel, help me pick.'

Daniel surveyed the vast array of fish in front of them, and tried to decide which one was least likely to eclipse him in size by the year's end. Their scales ranged from bright yellow in hue to an almost deep red.

'How about that one?' he said, and pointed to a fish on the red end of the spectrum. It was practically crimson, marred only by a white spot near its gills. It was also the smallest one there.

Keira marvelled at their new pet as she took the bag. 'Wow, look at him,' she said, twirling her finger to try catch its attention. 'Have you ever seen a red goldfish before? And look at his *wittle* spot. Aw he's so cute, what will we call him?'

'How do you know it's a him?' Daniel asked as they walked away from the stand. 'Not very progressive of you. It might not conform to our society's stance on gender-norms.'

'I don't think he knows what gender is, Daniel, and I don't think you care either. But fine, have it your way, we'll call it *they* for now, but they still need a name.'

Daniel rolled his eyes. 'Jesus Christ, what have I started?' He leaned in for a closer look at the fish. 'I don't know, Spot?'

'Spot's no name for a fish,' Keira said, 'especially for the paragon of social justice this one will be. *They* need to be something grand, like Jezebel.'

'Oh shut up,' Daniel said. They were nearing the car now, and Keira still hadn't noticed the bulge in his pocket. 'You decide then.'

'God, I hope you're this easy when it comes to the real thing,' Keira said, still staring through the plastic bag at the fish.

Daniel's stomach fluttered, and he slowed in his tracks. 'What do you mean?'

'What?' Keira asked, and looked up at him. Her eyes widened. 'Wait, what did I say?'

The flutter became a whirlwind, and he was aware of his increased heartbeat. 'You said, "God, I hope you're this easy when it comes to the real thing."'

Keira's mouth matched that of the fish now, bobbing up and down as it did. She closed it quickly when she saw how Daniel was staring at her, and tried to recover. 'Oh, I, eh, I just meant–'

Daniel's tongue was very dry. 'Keira, are you pregnant?'

Keira's mouth fell back open, and it seemed she'd forgotten how to close it.

Daniel put a soft hand on her arm, and swallowed. 'Well?'

Keira looked up at him, and gulped. 'Yes?'

'"Yes?"' Daniel repeated. 'Yes, you are?'

'Yes,' Keira nodded, as her eyes blurred. 'Yes I am.'

The next thing he knew, Daniel was on his knees, the ring out of his pocket and into his hands. 'Keira will you marry me?'

Keira's eyes bulged like great balloons as the evening sun cast her features red, and she swallowed again. 'Yes?'

'Yes?' Daniel asked. He'd never known his heart to beat so fast, never knew it could.

'Yes,' Keira said, and this time, there was no question about it. Daniel rose and she fell into his chest, wrapped her arms around him. She didn't even take the ring. 'Yes, yes, yes.'

Daniel gently shoved her away and slipped it onto her finger. The glow of the sun sparkled off the diamond's surface and onto the goldfish's white spot, shining it brilliant white against its deep shade of red.

'How long have you known?' Daniel asked as he brushed the hair away from her tear-streaked face.

'About three weeks,' Keira said. She was trying very hard not to cry. 'So it's been about six.' Another look down at the ring and she could stop herself no longer, but through her tears she smiled, the most beautiful, contented smile that ever was. 'How long have you?'

'About six weeks,' Daniel said softly, awestruck. The day they'd gone to the famine road. He'd known walking home, the next chance he got... 'I was just waiting for –'

'The right moment to tell you,' Keira said, and looked down at the little fish again.

20

'Well, the right moment to ask.'

'I actually quite like the name Spot,' she said, unable to take her eyes off the creature.

'Well,' Daniel breathed, 'if I'd known it'd be this easy, I'd have done away with the ring altogether.'

'Oh shut up,' Keira said. Finally, she looked away from the fish and up again at Daniel. 'Why haven't you kissed me yet?' she asked.

So he did.

21

Cold. Or rather, the lack of it. That was the only thing telling Daniel he must be asleep right now, because if he were really here, outside in the middle of the night, wearing nothing but his underwear, then he'd be cold. Freezing.

What was he doing here?

He looked up and down the length of the wooded road, unable to tell beginning from end. A lot of the time when Daniel dreamed, he saw himself in third person, like watching a film. It was nothing like that now, he really could have been there. Except for the cold.

A voice, laughter, and Daniel whipped his head around. In the wan light of the moon, the trees cast long shadows, and obscured what lay beyond. There was no way of telling where the noise had come from, but something about it felt distantly familiar, like he'd heard it before. Or was still to hear it yet.

Hands clamped over his eyes from behind, and he screamed.

'Daniel? Daniel wake up, you're okay. Can you hear me, Daniel? Wake up, it's okay.'

Daniel's eyes flicked open, awake, but he was not okay, nor could he speak. He lay with his back flat against the mattress, unable to move. The soft touch of Keira's arms rubbing against his chest was reassuring, but far away. Quite unlike the sensation of being pinned down, of knees against his chest, of breath right in his face, cold breath, and he could feel that cold now. He tried to scream again, to speak, but couldn't open his mouth. He was paralysed.

'Hey, it's okay. Are you listening? It's okay, I've got you.'

Keira leant in and hugged him, and it was only then Daniel realised he was shaking all over. Somehow, this snapped him out of it, and he came back to himself, managed to roll over so that he faced his wife.

'Hey,' he croaked.

'Hey,' Keira said, and stroked his stubble. 'You okay?'

Daniel nodded.

'Was it a bad one?'

He didn't answer right away. Already, the details of the dream were slipping away into the far part of the brain where thoughts went to die.

'I don't… think so,' he said at last.

'Okay, well come here anyway and I'll give you a spoon.'

Daniel did as he was told, his throat tight, and kissed Keira's hands as they wrapped around him. He felt like crying but didn't know why, and refused to allow himself.

From the plastic cot at the end of their bed, someone wasn't so self-conscious.

'Yikes,' Keira muttered at the high-pitched keen Rosanna let loose following the sounds of her parents.

'I'll get her,' Daniel said, but Keira's grip on his wrist stayed his leave.

'You sure?' she asked. 'I can do it, you look like you need the rest.'

Daniel looked at her and the ameliorative half-smile she offered. Lack of rest wasn't the reason she didn't want him to do it, he knew it and she knew it, but he shrugged all the same. 'If you want.'

Keira pecked him on the cheek and slipped out of bed, cooing at Rosanna as she lifted the wailing child out of her cot and into the hallway. Rather than close his eyes, Daniel rolled onto his back again and stared up at the ceiling.

No matter how hard he tried, he could never get Rosanna to stop crying. Keira, by all means, was a natural. Ten minutes at most, that was all it ever took, and the three of them would be sleeping again. Daniel's record before giving up and passing the torch stood at three hours and thirty-three minutes, and even that after Keira had twice offered to take over.

He got the sense the child didn't like him. Whether it was his squat, manly face, so unlike her beautiful mother's, his gruff voice, or something about his scent, he didn't know, but she reacted differently to him than her. She'd be laughing in her cot, and he'd look in to see what was so funny, and then she'd stop. She only did this for him, not for Keira, not for Keira's friend Amy, not even for Joe, who was terrified of the mere idea of children. Only for him.

Already the sounds were fading from the hallway, and Daniel reached over to his phone, flicked back to the page that he'd bookmarked of late. **Postnatal Depression – Signs and Symptoms**. He skimmed through them again. *Symptoms may include but are not limited to: inability to concentrate, loss of appetite, agitation, exhaustion, insomnia, mood swings, feelings of inadequacy, panic, feeling rejected by your baby, constantly worrying about your baby –*

It went on and on and on, but at no point did it come right out and say it, so at no point could Daniel allow himself to think it. But think it he did.

Sometimes he thought of leaving a comment, anonymously of course, but the last time anyone had replied to this particular forum was a little over four years ago, so his luck was probably out there. Even if it weren't though, if the comments were still active, he doubted he could have anyways. It was too terrible a thought, and to see it written down, at his own hand, well that would be the most terrible thing in the world.

Keira came back in then, Rosanna asleep on her shoulder and gave Daniel a tired smile. Daniel returned it, but it never reached his eyes. As Keira laid the child to rest, Daniel rolled back over onto his side and let himself be spooned again as he tried to fall asleep, but couldn't.

His mind danced around the symptom that was not there, and in the pit of his stomach, Daniel felt empty.

The list did not account for the absence of feeling.

20

Daniel stared at the empty Word document, as if doing so would will the words onto the page. When they didn't, he continued to stare.

Where had all his ideas gone? He seemed to remember they'd been countless back around the time his second novel, *Fire Flies*, was published. Now he could scarcely think of a sentence, let alone the plot for a new novel.

A click from behind him, followed by the sound of the attic stairs descending. Daniel suppressed the urge to groan. The only thing he hated more than his inability to write was people walking in on him in the midst of failing to do so.

'What is… it?'

Daniel's brow furrowed. The stairs were down, but there were no sounds from below.

'That you, Keira?'

A distant '*what?*' from the kitchen told him it wasn't. The creases in his forehead deepened, and he rose to shut the door, when the sound of plodding feet stilled him, and Rosanna's shiny blonde head popped into view.

'Hello!'

'Rosanna?' Daniel frowned as she bobbed over to him, thinking of the faulty latch and how difficult it was to properly hook onto. 'How did you…'

He trailed off to the tune of fresh footsteps on the staircase, followed by Keira with a stupid grin on her face.

'I'm sorry but that was too funny.'

'Hilarious,' Daniel said, and pretended to have the wind knocked out of him as Rosanna dumped herself in his lap.

'What are you doing?'

'Writing, honey.'

Keira stepped over to have a look at the screen. 'How're you getting on today?'

Daniel folded the laptop down before she could see the plain white page. 'Fine until you showed up.'

Keira blinked. 'Well, God forbid you'd want to spend time with your wife and daughter. Come on Rosie, let's head back downstairs. Your father has more important things to attend to.'

Daniel held out a hand to stop her. 'Hey it was just a joke, relax.'

'Oh, so funny. Look how much I'm laughing.'

'What, you mean like I did at yours?'

Keira's pursed lips spelled danger. 'You're right, wanting to surprise Dad at work is the same as telling Mum to fuck off.'

'Woah not in front of –'

'In front of who? Rosanna?' Keira held out a hand for the child now, who took it as she leapt back down from Daniel's lap. 'How would you know what to and what not to say in front of her? When was the last time you did anything together?'

Daniel stood up, a frown fully settled now. 'What do you mean? Earlier today I –'

'Besides plonking her down in front of the tv with a box of crayons and some paper so you can watch the match?'

Daniel glared at Keira, who gave it back just as well, before his eyes flicked to Rosanna, who'd taken refuge behind her mother's legs. His anger wilted.

'Okay, fine. I'll take her for a walk. Do you want to go for a walk, Rosanna?'

'Jesus Christ, Daniel, she's not a dog.'

'Oh for f– I can't win, can I?'

'It's not about winning! It's about spending time with your daughter!'

The staring match continued for a couple of moments before Keira puffed out her cheeks and shook her head. 'You know what? A walk might be good, actually. I'm sick of the sight of you.'

Daniel resisted the urge to respond, though plenty of scathing replies rushed through his head as he and Rosanna bundled up and made their way out of the secluded drive of what was once his

27

grandmother's home, now his. Here he'd been raised and here he'd stayed, ever since his parents died, on the fringes of Ballyfarreg, the nearby village where he'd used to, and Rosanna now, went to school. Much of the old famine workers that took part in Granny's stories had come from the village, or so she claimed, though whenever he'd broached the topic at school or otherwise, none else had ever heard of what he was talking about.

Theirs was a secluded spot, he and old Granny Cawley's. Far from town and village both, he'd had his own private world of trees and fields growing up, a picture-book landscape of the proverbial hill and dale, and it was past these that he and Rosanna walked, tucked into the side of the road.

Daniel sipped from his re-usable coffee mug, another devise of Keira's to annihilate plastic waste, world hunger, *et al*, and watched the way Rosanna's golden locks jounced against her shoulders as she waddled the way in front of them.

Too much of his time lately was spent staring at those golden locks, nothing at all like his black and Keira's shining brown. Not to mention her eyes. She took after Keira's mum, Mary, apparently, but Daniel continued to find himself looking.

'What's in here?' Rosanna asked, stopping before the old roped-off gate.

'Oh, we shouldn't go in –' Daniel began, but just as he did so, he felt the first droplets of rain nestle into his hair. A quick glance up at the sky signalled only worse to come, and home was twenty minutes away. The forest at least would provide some shelter. 'Alright, what the hell?'

Daniel set his mug down beside the gate and went about untying the knot, but a downward jolt to the frame raised his head, and he saw Rosanna had already clambered halfway over.

'Okay, okay, wait for me,' Daniel said, and hopped the gate in turn, abandoning his coffee for the time being. It was nearly finished anyways.

As his feet touched base with the stones for the first time in almost six years, Rosanna stared around in wonder.

'Woah. It's like Mozart.'

Daniel gave a bemused smile. 'How do you mean?'

'With the red sea. *KAPOW!*' Rosanna thrust her arms out to either side to accompany the cry, and turned back to Daniel. 'That's how he did it.'

The smile grew. 'Well, your heart's in the right place.'

'Oh I hope so,' Rosanna said solemnly, before wandering off ahead.

Daniel watched her go, and an easiness came over him that he hadn't known in some time, as she weaved in and out between the trees, not quite running, but not walking either, and certainly no trace of the waddle she'd had difficulty shaking from her toddler years.

'Having fun?' he asked, as she scrambled for a foothold on a nearby tree. 'Woah, careful now, don't fall –' but the words died on his tongue as he found himself staring at the girl raised two metres off the ground, perched in a Y-shaped seat. 'Since when did you get so good at climbing?'

Rosanna shrugged. 'It's easy, you just go up from the ground.'

'I suppose it is quite easy, when you put it like that. But is it just as easy to come down?'

'Sure,' Rosanna said, and leapt before Daniel had the chance to move.

His heart caught in his throat and his feet froze to the spot as she sailed through the air and landed unceremoniously on her rump in the grass.

'Jesus!' Daniel cried as the first wail escaped her lips, and he rushed to her side. 'Are you okay? Rosie, come here, are you –'

It was then he noticed Rosanna wasn't crying, she was laughing.

'See. Easy.'

For a moment, Daniel could only stare, no idea how to react. He knew he should scold her, warn her off ever doing something so reckless again, but even as he opened his mouth to do so, a barked laugh escaped instead, and he found himself rolling in the grass alongside her. By the time he'd finally recovered, an idea was brewing in his head.

After a few more minutes of amiable wandering, the sky above cleared up, and the two began their walk home, though unfortunately for Keira's great campaign to save the world he somehow lost his re-usable mug along the way, it just wasn't where he remembered leaving it. In any case, when at last they returned home, Daniel's spirits were higher than they'd been in a long time.

'What's got you so smiley?' Keira asked as the pair took off their coats.

Daniel told Rosanna to wash her hands after touching all those dirty trees, and when she ran off to the bathroom, he turned that smile on Keira.

'I know what I'm going to write about.'

Keira's eyebrows raised. 'You mean you didn't already?'

'I had a few things knocking around,' Daniel lied, 'but nothing as red-hot as this.'

'Well, Mr. Hot-shot, what is it you're going to write about?'

Daniel leaned in to kiss her forehead, and when he stepped back, his eyes were bright.

'Rosanna.'

19

Trips to the famine road became frequent. While Keira was at work, Daniel would swing out to the village in the afternoons to collect Rosanna from school, and on their way home they often stopped for a quick jaunt through the trees. After the third or fourth time, Daniel started bringing a note copy with him, to jot down any observations he had on her movements, and the way she interacted with the world around her. Little things to help with his writing, and harmless enough, or so he'd thought.

'What the hell is this?'

Daniel looked up from the tv, and saw that Keira held his notebook. 'What are you doing with that?'

'What am I – have you read this thing, Daniel?'

'Of course I've read it, I wrote it didn't I? Why are you going through my things?'

Keira paused only to glance over to where Rosanna was doing her homework at the kitchen table. 'Rosanna go to your room.'

Daniel clenched his jaw as the child did as she was told. Keira closed the door behind her.

'Why am I going through your things? Well sorry I didn't realise your bedside table was off-fucking-limits.' Her hands shook as she held the copy out in front of him, and her eyes were wild. 'Have you *seen* this thing?'

'What's wrong with it?'

'What's –' Keira bit her tongue as furious eyes flicked from person to page. '"*Tuesday, 2.46PM, She runs like a thing unleashed, freed from the laborious shackles of everyday life in such a way that when her hand wraps round branch and she ascends through the trees, nature and her become one.*"' She stopped to look at him.

'So?'

'So!' That had done it. Never before had the flipping of paper sounded so much like the cocking of a gun. '"*Thursday, 3.06PM, It's*

hard to describe the sense of awe that comes over one, watching her here. The confidence with which she weaves between the trees, vanishing one side of the road and reappearing just behind me on the other, how does she do it? Of course the blame can be laid with my inability to keep an eye on her at all times, but it's impossible not to get caught up in the scenery of the trees and the light and the wind
— " You're not even fucking watching her half the time!'

'Oh come on, of course I am. Haven't you ever heard of hamming things up for dramatic effect?'

'She's not your "dramatic effect" project Daniel! She's your daughter!' Keira threw the book at him, and it bounced against his chest before falling open on his lap. 'Look at that thing. Read the page right in front of you. Lucky dip. You're treating her like she's some sort of patient.'

Daniel glanced down at the page, saw the word *ethereal* and immediately disregarded reading it aloud. 'I don't see what the big deal is. You wanted me to spend more alone time with her, so I am.'

'I wanted you play games with her, help her with her homework, bring her for ice-cream. I don't want you writing down every single thing she does so that you can warp her into the protagonist of your next bloody book. She's your *daughter*, Daniel.'

'That's not what I'm doing.'

'Isn't it?'

'No. Like I said before, it's going to be a collection of –'

'Of all the stories your granny used to tell you, right. The same granny who thought it would be a wonderful idea to emotionally scar you the day after your parents died. What a terrific role model, Daniel, really.'

'Will you ease off? I don't see what that has to do with anything. Yeah she was kind of mental but she told some cool stories, what's wrong with writing them down?'

'Is that how you want people to remember you? *"Kind of mental but he told some cool stories?"* Because that's what's happening. What you're doing is mental. That *thing* is mental.'

'I don't –'

'What happens to Rosanna, in your story?'

Daniel blinked. 'What?'

'In your collection. What happens with her? Do you kill her off? Feed her to the faeries? What are you writing all that down for, anyways?'

'I don't know yet, I haven't decided. Nothing like that though, Jesus.'

'Do you swear?'

'What?'

'Do you swear that it's nothing like that? Because I swear to you Daniel, if I read what you've written and I see *any* mention of any sort of harm coming to the poor girl you've chose to represent our daughter then... then...'

'Hey, woah, it's alright.' Daniel rose from the couch.

Keira's frame was stiff in his embrace. 'I don't want you going back there. You or her. And I want *this* –' she motioned at the notebook '– to stop.'

Daniel nodded, pressed his chin against her hair. 'Okay,' he said, 'I'll stop, I promise.'

'Okay,' Keira said, and the entire weight went out of her as she sagged into him. 'Thank you.'

'It's alright,' Daniel said, rubbing the small of her back, and it was.

He had what he needed already.

18

There are few things in life as wondrous as the spirit of a child, and what's more, they know this. They watch her frolic through the trees and the leaves, past branch and bramble, they watch her, and they wait. They need only wait, for they know their time will –

Click!

Daniel's shoulders tightened as the attic stairs unfolded behind him. Just as he was starting to get into things, when else could ever make for another one of Keira's hilarious surprises? It was always the moment things started to flow that she…

No footsteps came, adult or child, and it was then Daniel remembered that Keira was at work, Rosanna at school, and he was alone in the house.

His eyes settled on the little square hole that marked the border between his professional and private life, or at least pertained to. It remained that, a hole, on the other side of which something had caused this border to open.

Thoughts of the faulty latch were at the forefront of Daniel's mind as he rose to inspect the disturbance, but that didn't make much sense. The latch caused the stairs to stick, not descend. It was what made them so bloody difficult to open, and the reason behind Keira's little trick the last day. Maybe she was home early.

'Keira? That you?'

No response was forthcoming, and the stairs led down to an empty hallway. Daniel's irritation at being interrupted waned, replaced by prickles of unease.

'Is there anyone down there?'

Silence. If there were someone downstairs who wanted to make themselves known to Daniel, then they would have done so already. He didn't so much like the alternative, unless it was Keira hiding out on him again. It was Friday after all, and almost two o'clock, she might have made it home early. If she hadn't, then it was up to Daniel to figure out if someone else had. Back to his desk, he took out the pen-knife he kept in the side-drawer. Primarily used as a bottle-opener, he inched his way down the stairs, and hoped it stayed like that.

'Hello?'

His voice echoed in the narrow hallway, so that the only reply was his own. This was getting ridiculous now, there clearly wasn't anyone here, he should go back to his writing while he still had the house to himself, except…

Except what if he didn't?

It was less out of fear than frustration that Daniel rolled the knot out of his back and stormed down the hallway, barging open doors to Rosanna's room, the bathroom, and he and Keira's bedroom as he went. When, of course, all came up blank, he shook his head and headed for the kitchen to make a cup of tea and cool off, where he stopped.

There, on the middle of the table, one was already made.

Steam rose from its top, freshly prepared, but that wasn't what caught Daniel's attention, not right away, that wasn't what made his balls drop and his heart soar. No, it was the mug that did that.

Daniel floated forward to inspect it, in a daze, and gathered it in his hands so that there could be no doubt. It was the re-usable cup he'd lost on the famine road.

A cold stole through him as he froze to the spot, staring, along with the distant feeling of wispy fingers reaching for his eyes, creeping ever so slowly forward until –

The front door crunched open, and re-instilled Daniel's ability to move.

'Daniel, we're back!'

Oh thank Christ. He hadn't even been aware of his heartbeat until that moment, but it burned now with the fear of an Orange bonfire. He turned with the cup in his hand to face wife and daughter, knowing he could never explain but glad at least to be able to share in the madness, when he saw that it wasn't his daughter that accompanied Keira.

'Oh. Amy. Hello. How are you?'

*

As Keira and Amy chatted over him at the kitchen table, Daniel tried to work out if he'd been imagining things. Not the cup of tea, that was real enough, the two women had even watched in bemusement as he'd poured it down the sink, but rather the events leading to the cup of tea's being there. As the front door opened, he'd frozen, paralysed, unable to move anything except his eyes. Just like in his dreams.

Was he sleepwalking? Had he made the tea in his sleep? Doubtless, he could, he drank more than five cups a day, but he didn't believe that. Everything leading up to it had been so visceral, so real, but then, so were the night-terrors. Or the sleep-terrors, he supposed he should call them, they weren't restricted to night.

Even if he had dreamed it, that didn't explain the cup. It had been missing for weeks, he knew as much because Keira had asked for it recently to bring into work, and after he combed the forest floor on one of his latest trips with Rosanna, he'd had to tell her he'd lost it. So what the hell was it doing in the sink?

Daniel downed his tea, a fresh mug, one that he was sure he'd made for himself. If it had been a dream, then wasn't falling asleep, and dreaming it all, better than the alternative? The only problem was, he didn't see at what point that could have happened.

He'd woken up, eaten, went upstairs to do some writing, heard the click some hours later, and now here he was.

But if he hadn't fallen asleep, where did that leave him? Was he losing his mind? He'd like to think madness would be a little more grandiose than that. Or, could it be that someone who had similarly lost it had just happened upon his re-usable mug, somehow recognised it as his, and rather than do the somewhat rational thing of returning it to him – or the even more rational thing of just leaving it there – they'd broken into his house, made some tea in the cup, opened the stairs to his attic, and left undetected. Between that and falling asleep at his desk, Daniel knew which one he'd rather believe.

'Who's picking up Rosanna?' he asked abruptly, stung by the clock into realising what time it was.

Keira gave him a funny look as she paused her conversation with Amy. 'She's at Sam's house, I told you that already.'

Sam. He was the one with the… No wait, Sam was a girl. Or was she? He? Daniel shook his head. He had to stop overthinking things.

'Are you okay?' Keira asked. 'You look a bit pale.'

'Fine, yeah, fine… yeah.' Daniel sipped from his tea lest he find himself endlessly repeating the two words.

'Have you been listening to what Amy's saying?'

Daniel looked over to where Amy gave an embarrassed smile, her attention focused on the contents of her cup. 'No, sorry, I was away… no I didn't, what were you saying?'

39

'They want to make the movie,' Amy said, not meeting Daniel's eyes.

'Wow,' he blinked. 'That's fantastic. Incredible, really. Well done.' He was careful not to let the flash of envy show in either his face or voice.

'And they want to keep her on as executive producer,' Keira said.

'Wow,' Daniel repeated, as Amy's smile tightened slightly. He wondered if she knew, if she remembered.

'Isn't it amazing?' Keira grinned wildly as she shook Amy's arm. 'God knows you've deserved it. Does this mean you'll get to go on set?'

'Yeah, they're starting filming in the new year. The plan is to film the first scene on the main beach in Ballyfarreg, you know, where they find her. They said I could tag along if I like.'

'Do they have a cast and all already figured out?' Keira asked.

'Yeah I think so, no-one I've ever heard of though. Supposedly the boy is very good, from what I've been told, but they want to age him up from eight to thirteen, which I don't know how I feel about.'

'Well a thirteen year old certainly doesn't have the same innocence,' Keira said.

'That was my point exactly.'

Daniel felt himself drifting out of the conversation. He hadn't read Amy's book, why did they think he'd suddenly care now that it was being made into a film? Well, that wasn't strictly true. He did care, in the sense that she had a movie deal and he didn't, but that was as much as he'd ever allow himself to think about Amy. Any more, and he was apt to get a little angry.

'What time was Rosanna meant to be staying at Sam's until?' Daniel cut in, grinding their conversation to a halt once more. 'I might pick up some bits and get her on the way out. Sam lives in town, right?'

'No…' Keira said. 'He lives in the village, but if you need to bop to the shops don't let us keep you.'

'Right so.' Daniel rose, aware that he was bristling and hating himself for it. When it had been his decision to leave, he'd been all for it, get him the hell out of this kitchen, but the way Keira had been so quick to jump on board, it was almost like she wanted him g–

He was doing it again. Stop overthinking, and everything would be alright.

*

Up through the floorboards wafted the muffled sounds of Keira and Amy hugging each other goodbye, and Daniel at last closed the lid on his laptop. His laptop, but not his novel. That remained exactly where he'd left it this afternoon, still frozen on the half-sentence *"they know their time will –"*

He'd thought about finishing it, after he'd picked Rosanna up, it just needed the one word after all, but rather than this he cracked open the beer he'd gotten alongside, so while Keira was busy entertaining Amy, and Rosanna was off doing whatever it was she did when neither parent was looking, he sat up here pretending to write, and drank.

He couldn't stop thinking about the cup.

Who had put it there? And what if he'd drank the tea, instead of pouring it down the sink? Was someone trying to poison him? He'd got his fair share of hate mail in response to one or two particularly gruesome moments in the wake of his first novel, but those had died down years ago, and everyone knew death threats nowadays were the kind of thing you threw around Twitter and Instagram after your football team lost, so that your tiny dick could feel *that* much bigger. No-one ever acted on them. Right?

It would be a pretty clumsy way to try and kill someone, or so he'd thought, but then he drank some more, and kept drinking, and eventually came to the conclusion that it wasn't clumsy, it was brilliant. Sneak in just as the wife is about to run home, poison the tea, leave it out for him on the table, and witness the sight and savour the sound as countless Christian mothers climax to his demise.

Keira was watching the television when Daniel came back downstairs, trying his damnedest not to walk like a sailor. She had a stack of copies on the couch beside her and a pen in her hand. She didn't look up when he walked in.

'Dinner duty you or me?' Daniel asked, all in one breath to hide the slur. 'I got a bunch of chicken there earlier.'

'I'm not hungry.'

42

Daniel squinted at the kitchen clock as the room spun around him. 'It's not even seven, you will be. What you want?'

'I had a big lunch.'

Her tone spelled trouble, while Daniel's spelled D-R-U-N-K. Not a happy combo. 'What did you have?'

'Food.'

Daniel paused halfway in reaching for the fridge and grimaced. Dare he ask?

'Everything alright?'

'Yep, everything's fine.'

The grimace became a wince, and Daniel shuffled over to the couch. It was only then he noticed Rosanna on the floor in front, colouring away.

'You sure?'

Keira looked up at him for a moment, then rolled her eyes and shook her head. 'God you're just... you're so infuriating at times.'

Wince grew to frown as Daniel sat on the couch's arm. 'How do you mean?'

'Never mind, just go have another beer, it's fine.'

His stomach sank. 'Is this about Amy?'

'Just leave it.' Keira reached for a copy.

'Why are you getting angry at me? You know I don't like her, I only put up with her because –'

Keira flapped her arms down on the couch 'Is that what you call putting up with her? Not listening to a word she says? Not

43

talking to her at all, or me for that matter. And then going off on a beer-run with the pretence of picking up your daughter. Is that what you'd call it? Jesus Christ Daniel, you're such a fucking child.'

Daniel's eyes flicked across to Rosanna at this last part, but she didn't appear to have noticed. He turned back to Keira. 'I'm a child, am I? Well at least I don't still hang around with my college fuck-toy.'

'Oh grow up Daniel, that was nearly fifteen years ago.'

'What about back in Yeats's?' Daniel asked. Yeats's was the name of the apartment complex where Keira and Amy had lived together before she moved in with Daniel. 'Don't you go giving out to me over a few beers. At least I don't try to crawl into any of my friend's beds in that state.'

'How the hell is that my fault? Amy has apologised for that again and again –'

'Not to me!'

'How would you know? You never fucking listen to her.'

'I –' Daniel stopped. Rosanna was staring up at the two of them, Keira's eyes red and tired, his own face flushed and angry. A silence fell between them.

Keira broke it first. 'Hey sweetie,' she said, and wiped at her eyes, 'what were you drawing?'

Rosanna held the sketchpad up without a word.

'Wow, that's a really nice tree. Good job.'

Daniel watched as Keira bent to pick her up, a lump in his throat.

'Why don't you show me the rest of your drawings? Come on, let's go to your room.'

She didn't look at him as the two went out the kitchen door, and he didn't try to stop her.

Dinner ended up being chicken curry, not that there'd been much choice, he'd bought 700g of the stuff earlier when they already had a kilogramme sitting in the fridge. No wonder she'd seen through him.

As he scrubbed away at the clean-up then, his eyes settled on the reusable cup once more, still in the sink. He hadn't told her about it yet, and could hardly do so now. At best it would sound like an excuse, at worst...

The bed was empty when he got there, after another beer or three. Keira stayed in Rosanna's room for the evening, and showed no signs of coming out. Daniel stripped off his clothes and hopped into the cold bed, too large for one person on their own.

He fell asleep staring at the ceiling.

17

Daniel woke to an empty bed, covered in sweat, the memory of what caused it already gone, but the rapid beat of his heart yet to reach the same conclusion.

Dread seeped out of him like vapour off to meet the clouds as he rose to join his family, but condensed again at the kitchen door.

Along with his troubled sleep, the finer details of yesterday's argument had slipped his mind, though his head brewed a storm.

A peep through the door showed Keira and Rosanna both on the couch, mother's arm slung round daughter as cartoons played on the television. Daniel took a deep breath and went in.

'Morning,' he said as he tossed a few flakes into Spot's fishbowl.

'Afternoon,' Keira murmured back, eyes only for the tv.

'Sleep alright?'

'Fine.'

The cloying stink of sweat still upon him, that she didn't ask after his own had to be intentional.

'I was thinking of going for a run later, clear the head. Been a bit foggy.'

'Eight beers will do that to you.'

Daniel's eyes flicked to the bin. Had she been counting?

'Well, it's a bit cold out there anyway. You got any under-armour shirts I can borrow?'

Keira did look at him then, up and down, eyes settling most notably in the midriff, where his stomach bulged comfortably over the band of his underwear.

'I don't think they'll fit.'

Staring at himself in the bathroom mirror, each line of fat now accentuated by a skin-tight fluorescent pink undershirt, Daniel had to concede that she was right. Not that this stopped him from boldly marching back into the kitchen with hands on hips.

'What do you think?'

He thought he saw the hint of a smile on Keira's face before she turned away again.

'Dashing.'

There was something to be said for how wearing the right clothes put you in the right mood, and Daniel found himself hopping about on the spot, filled with energy. 'Might go now actually, feel like I could go for ten miles.'

'Ten minutes, you mean.'

'I'm going to do twice that now, just to prove you wrong.'

Keira rolled her eyes. 'Aren't you going to have breakfast first? Long way to go on an empty stomach is twenty minutes.'

At some point, Daniel had started shadow-boxing, much to Rosanna's fascination. 'I'll get my food out there. Worms to catch and all that.'

'Don't say it like that.'

'Like what?'

'You know–' Keira was cut off as Daniel kissed her cheek.

'Love you,' he said as he left the kitchen and Keira grumbled her response. To Rosanna, he winked.

To add to the pink undershirt, Daniel wore an old Ireland jersey from the ill-fated Korea campaign, a pair of swimming shorts, and his normal everyday trainers. Far from the essential running collection, the mish-mash elevated rather than deterred his mood. Nothing wrong with the neighbours thinking he was a little tapped. If anything, it added to his mad-writer aesthetic.

This wave of good cheer lasted all of two minutes, until he was pretty sure he was going to die, and very sure he was about to throw up. When neither happened and the blackspots in his vision cleared, Daniel concluded that if he were to last twenty minutes out of the house, he was going to have to do so walking.

As he walked, deafened by the loud silence of country life, his thoughts returned, yet again, to the cup. He wished that they didn't, more than anything he wanted to shove the image of that stupid plastic greenwashing mug from existence, but he couldn't. How could he? A mug that *he'd* lost had somehow found its way back to his kitchen table, tea ready-made and all. Was he just supposed to ignore that?

Daniel felt the tingle in his neck before he saw the cracked-white paint of the old road's gate, but he wasn't sure which gave him pause. Granny Cawley, now there was someone who'd have a lot to say about what happened yesterday. That he'd lost the mug just the other side of that gate had not slipped his mind.

There was no need to look both ways as Daniel crossed the road, so he didn't. He ran his fingers across the length of frayed rope that had kept the gate shut for so many years, and wondered, not for the first time, who had put it there?

He held the rope in his grip, and hesitated. He knew this was bizarre, but in the light of what happened, what harm in checking the place out? Maybe he'd see once and for all if there was a clearing at the end of the forest. Daniel moved to undo the knot, when a gust of wind blew some loose dust up from the stones, and he recoiled, sneezing.

Then he sneezed again, and again, and again. When it became clear that this wasn't a simple phase but a running gauntlet, Daniel staggered back from the gate and had to make the uncomfortable journey home, nose screaming all the while, and his hands were caked the same colour as his jersey by the time he reached it.

'Hey, twenty-seven minutes, I'm imp- Jesus, what's wrong with you?'

Daniel shook his head as he stumbled over to the sink, head thundering as his nose launched another tirade.

'What, did you suddenly get hay-fever or something, what's going on?'

Daniel tilted his head upside down so that water flowed into both nostrils, then pulled away, spluttering. He motioned to Keira for a tissue, and when at last it was presented to him and his nose cleared, a blade of grass lay amongst the mucus and paper.

'Christ,' Daniel muttered at last, his blood finally having remembered there were other places to store itself than his head, and he sank down onto the couch.

'What the hell was that?'

'Grass…' Daniel wheezed. Between the running and the sneezing, he was utterly exhausted. 'Got stuck… in my nose. Couldn't… pick it out.'

'Nice run then?'

Daniel nodded, gasping, only just seeing that Rosanna was in the room too. She glanced up from her book, and gave him an odd look with her orange-hazel eyes. Daniel found himself frowning back in turn. Why was he the only one who thought they looked so strange?

'Earth to Daniel?'

'What? Oh right, lovely yeah, apart from the whole thinking I was about to die part.'

'Really? I find those parts to be the most fun.'

Daniel turned his frown on her now, as his lungs slowly refilled. 'Listen, about yesterday…'

Keira's smile slipped. 'What about it?'

'Sorry for going off on you like that, and for not… you know… making an effort around Amy and stuff.'

'Okay.'

Daniel sighed. 'And I'm sorry I used –' he nodded at Rosanna, nose buried in her book once more '– as an excuse to get away. I shouldn't have done that.'

'To get away and buy beer.'

'Yes, to get away and buy beer. It won't happen again, I promise.'

'Which won't?' Keira asked, plonking herself on the couch beside him. 'You've listed about three things there.'

'None of them… or, all of them,' Daniel said. He furrowed his brows. 'Any of them? *Not* any of them. Not any of them will happen again.'

'Hmm, I'm not convinced,' Keira said, but she scooched over to lean against him. 'Find me another synonym there, go on.'

'Oh shut up,' Daniel said, 'that's all I've been doing recently, my brain is fried. Negatory to the power of–'

'Fine, fine, I believe you. Nerd.'

'Those aren't even nerdy words!'

Keira shrugged. 'Sounds like something a nerd would say.'

Daniel huffed good-humouredly as he slung an arm around her shoulder, and they settled in for some good old, terribly modern, Sunday television.

'You know it's funny that, about the grass.'

Daniel barely heard, so transfixed was he by the Chaser's jowls. 'What is?'

'The way it came out with your snot like that,' Keira said, nestling her head against him. 'It's just like the stories.'

Daniel swallowed and nodded, the endorphins he'd fostered on his run fatherless once more. *Just like the stories.*

*

Staring at the ceiling had become something of a pastime for Daniel, something to keep him, well, entertained wasn't the right word, but at least occupied in the black of night when sleep refused to visit. Water-stains older than himself painted the bedroom sky a litany of shapes and colours and, strangely, made him thirsty.

Daniel slipped his numb arm out from under Keira's sleeping head, and tiptoed over to the kitchen, nipples fit to slice through his t-shirt from the cold. As water filled the glass, he wondered if he should give up on the whole sleeping endeavour and simply head upstairs, crack on with tomorrow's writing.

It was something he only half-considered. While insomnia seemed to be a great motivating tool for others, he'd yet to harness this borrowed energy for himself, and so he headed back to the bedroom. Or at least, he meant to.

The attic stairs blocked his path.

Daniel stared at them for a moment, all the while offering the ghosts in the hallway his best owl impression, and, entirely less than satisfied that he was alone, walked to their base. The latch was broken, simple as. If he'd needed any more proof after the last day, here it was.

But Daniel, you checked the latch yourself, it causes the stairs to stick, not fall open, remember?

Unable to silence his thoughts nor the beat of his heart in his ears, Daniel peered into the empty space at the stairs' top, and wondered if he imagined more than felt the cold breeze that draughted down it. Not for the first time since waking, his nipples answered the question for him.

A quick glance back toward the bedroom – sleep was hardly an option now, anyway – Daniel ascended the stairs. Far from a boisterous child, or indeed man, Daniel had never been the kind to boldly proclaim in front of a group that he was not afraid of the dark. Growing up in a house like this, an old cottage whose original foundations pre-dated the State, darkness lurked in every corner, and shadows danced. Gaps behind couches became crevices, where you could fall into and never return, if you weren't careful, and the living room hearth was the beacon of light around which you crowded, and were safe.

Daniel needed no reminding that there was no such hearth in the attic, but luckily for him a little something called electricity finally connected the entire homestead sometime around his ninth birthday, and he flicked the attic light now and... and he flicked the attic light now... he *flicked*...

Daniel stepped back from the wall, still shrouded in night. Upstairs it was closer, tighter. The walls were thin and the wind conniving, licking his exposed limbs as he stumbled blindly for his laptop, wary of all sorts of clefts and pitfalls that existed only in his mind's eye, which, for the time being, saw just as much as his real ones.

The knots in his back began to tighten as he took another step forward and reached for his desk to steady himself, came away only with clean air. It should not be this dark. There was a blind down over the window, meant more to keep the heat in than the light out, but even on the blackest nights, its outline shone with the white of the moon. Of that square panel, Daniel saw no more sign than his two hands in front of him, and, the fear in him now, he turned back the way he came, only to find it was no different than the way he'd been facing.

The hole in the ground was gone. The stairs were gone. The floor, it seemed, was gone. In a small black box high in the foothills of Ballyfarreg, time fell away, and as Daniel felt the first snaky tendrils of breath, ice across his young neck's veins, his body turned to stone, and there was no way he could scream.

16

Daniel chewed his cereal in silence, he the last to eat, and he was aware of every crunch.

'Would you be up for heading into town for lunch later?' Keira asked. 'Get out of the house for a couple hours.'

Daniel nodded. 'Sure, yeah.' He hadn't told her about last night.

'Where do you want to go?'

Daniel turned to her, and gazing into those welcome blue eyes, he tried to work up some resolve. Now was as good a time as any. 'Have you ever known me to sleepwalk?'

'What?'

'Just that. I know I get my bad dreams and the paralysis and all, but I don't ever remember being much of a sleepwalker. Have you noticed anything like that?'

'Don't you think I would have mentioned it if I did? Why, what's up?'

Daniel sighed. The circles under his eyes spoke of forts. 'I don't know, I feel weird. Offbeat. Last night I dreamt, or at least I thought I dreamt, that the attic stairs had come down by themselves again and when I went up to check –'

54

'Wait, what do you mean *again*?'

'Right. See they came down like that before, on Friday when I was here by myself, only when I went downstairs…' he trailed off. Actually saying it aloud, it sounded silly, like it couldn't have possibly happened in reality.

'Only when you went downstairs…?'

'Promise you won't laugh? Or that you won't think I'm crazy?'

'I mean, yeah I guess. You're kind of scaring me a bit –'

'There was a cup on the table when I came down. A cup of tea, already made in that reusable mug you got me, only… only I lost the mug a couple weeks back, and I remember because you were asking me for it and –'

'Hold on, what mug is this?'

'You know, the green one you got a while back, to save the turtles and all that. Camo pattern.'

Keira frowned. 'Vaguely… I don't know, maybe. I don't remember asking you for it.'

Daniel frowned in turn. 'What do you mean you don't remember asking for it? I specifically went back to the forest and combed the whole place front and back so I could find it for you.'

Keira stared at him blankly.

Daniel rose with a grunt. 'I'll show you.' He went over to the cabinet where they kept mugs of all race and gender, no discrimination here, and paused. 'Alright, very funny, where is it?' When he realised that Keira's wide-eyed disbelief was not an act, his

55

stomach dropped, and he swallowed. 'How well are you holding to that promise?'

'Well I'm not laughing, am I? Are you alright? You're very pale, I think you should sit down.'

Daniel did as he was bid, sank back into the chair, shaking his head. 'But it wasn't just the mug,' he muttered.

'What was that?'

'Last night.' He looked up at her. 'The whole sleepwalking thing I was on about. I dreamt I went to get a glass of water, or again, I *thought* I dreamt it, only when I came back into the hall, the stairs were down, like they had been before when I found the mug, or… or when I thought I'd found the mug, so I went up – I don't remember why, to do some writing or something – only I couldn't see anything and it was so dark and so cold and then there were all these hands on me and breathing and I couldn't see anything and –'

'Woah, woah, hey. Take a deep breath, you're okay.'

Daniel nodded, took a swig of water too, and cleared his head. 'I woke up in bed, then, but not right away. There's an empty space in my memory, but I must have come back down. At first I thought it was a dream, but when I went back up this morning there was a smashed pint glass on the floor.'

Keira's forehead creased. 'Hardly. I would have heard that.'

'That's what I thought too, but then if you didn't notice me get up then who's to say that you'd hear –'

'Daniel, listen to me. I didn't hear you get up, because you didn't get up. I didn't exactly have a great sleep myself last night, and I was awake for most of it. You were there with me right alongside, Daniel, and I'm glad you were.'

'But… what about the glass?'

Keira's expression went from sympathetic to a little less so. 'I mean, don't you think it's more likely you dropped the glass after your whole one-man party the last night? You didn't go up to write yesterday, after all.'

Daniel swallowed. 'Right.'

'Are you okay, Daniel?'

Keira's light blue eyes were like mirrors of his own, and Daniel saw himself too well in them. He ran a hand down his face. 'I don't know. Probably, yeah. It's just this new book –'

'Will you relax about this book, please? Jesus, Daniel, it's not like we need the money, or that there's anyone banging on your door to get it done.'

'I know, I know. I just feel like I've something special here and –'

'Yeah, you do have something special. Us.'

As if she'd heard her mother's words, Rosanna came bounding into the room, hand to shoulder caked in thick green paint, with a couple of swirls on her cheeks for good measure. 'Look, I'm a Martian!'

Daniel couldn't help but snort at Keira's stupefied expression. 'Just as it was all getting a bit profound.'

'Well,' Keira said, 'seeing as you think it's so funny, you can be the one to clean her and get her ready for lunch. No Martians allowed.'

Doing so proved exceptionally more difficult than either Daniel or Keira could have envisioned, with the deep green globules resistant to all types of swabbing, from cotton to toothbrush, and it ended up being a two-parent job.

'How did you get so much of it in your hair?' Keira asked. 'It's matted right into the scalp.'

Rosanna shrugged 'I was itchy.'

'Where did you even get the paint?' Daniel asked.

'In the shed.'

Daniel and Keira exchanged glances. There was all sorts of crap in that shed, from paint cans to old books, to Granny Cawley's collection of rabbits' feet, horseshoes, dreamcatchers, and various other miscellaneous madness, not to mention the numerous hammers, saws, and helpful slathering of likely undetected carbon monoxide.

'Best lock it.'

'You think?'

Once inside, however, Daniel had a little meander throughout the meagre confines of the wooden walls, and found himself peering through an album marked *Martin & Helen's Wedding, June 18th 1982*. It felt weird, seeing these strangers' faces, and knowing they were the ones who'd given him life. He'd only been four when they died, and his mother's face merged with his Granny's over the years, so that there wasn't much left. Of his father, he'd had no face at all.

'I found this,' Daniel said as Keira let the murkish water drain out of the tub.

'Oh. Oh wow. Let me have a look.'

Daniel found he had to resist the urge to bite his nails as he watched Keira flick through the photos, as if he could somehow be judged for them.

'Your mum was very pretty.'

Daniel nodded. 'Blonde, too.'

'What does that have to do with anything?'

Daniel flicked his head in the direction of Rosanna's room. 'Oh, you know.'

Keira rolled her eyes. 'Oh will you give over about her bloody hair? It was green ten minutes ago.'

Daniel shrugged. 'Just nice to know the odds that you cheated on me have gone considerably down.'

'Shut up, you know I would never.' She paused, frowning down at the page. 'Are you sure you can say the same for your own mother, though? Your dad looks nothing like you.'

'What? Show me that.'

'Nah.' Keira closed the book, hugged it to herself.

'Wow, you're really gonna do the whole "you just found pictures of your long-dead parents that you didn't know existed but because you called my fidelity into question I shall not only not let you see them but also try and suggest that you too are born out of illegitimacy" play?'

'Something like that, yeah.'

Daniel grinned. 'A classic. Now, what's for lunch?'

*

Lunch was the Wok House, and between the three of them they split a king prawn curry, chicken skewers, and a spice bag. When it had all been presented in individual bowls the size of saucepans, Daniel would have been surprised if five people had been able to eat everything in front of them. Keira had no such reservations.

'Jesus Christ, will you leave some for me,' Daniel said as another forkful of rice disappeared down her throat.

'Snooze you lose,' Keira said, her voice muffled by little bits of chicken.

'Charming.'

His phone buzzed then, and Daniel eyed it to see he had a text from Joe.

Pints tonight. Go on.

Daniel looked at it for a moment before putting it away. Of course he wanted to go for pints – who the hell didn't? – but he might be best served staying away from the drink for the next while, especially after recent events. Still, it would be nice to see Joe…

'Do we need anything else while we're in town, or are we going straight home after this?'

'Are you incapable of being out of there for more than five minutes?' Keira asked through a mouthful of chips. 'We just got here.'

Rosanna took a piece of chicken off the plate, chewed it briefly, then put the rest of it back where she got it and leaned back in her chair. Keira promptly picked up the half-eaten piece and finished the job.

Daniel frowned at this little sequence. 'Well what do you want to do then? Besides eat.'

Keira shot him a piercing look. 'What's that supposed to –'

'Nothing. Ow! I said nothing. Stop!'

Keira released her pinch with a grin. 'I don't know. We could go to the cinema or something.'

Rosanna's head shot up. 'I want to go to the cimena.'

'Alright, I'll go up and pay,' Daniel said to Keira, 'you check what's on.'

He did as much, the sum total more than half of what he'd pay for a week's grocery shopping, and when he came back the pair had a suggestion ready.

'The *Incredibles 2*?' Keira asked, and Rosanna nodded her head approvingly.

'Has she seen the first one?'

'Yes!' Rosanna declared, but that didn't exactly mean much.

Keira shrugged. 'Does it matter?'

'Fair enough, will we get walking then?'

'Hang on, I'm not finished,' Keira said, and Daniel saw there were four chips left. He'd only had about five himself.

'Let me help you with that,' he said, and grabbed the lot in one big fistful and shoved it into his gob, unaware of the hidden chili stashed amongst them. Rosanna giggled as he stuck out his tongue and fanned his mouth. 'Hot!'

'Great observation,' Keira said. 'You're buying me popcorn for that.'

'How can you still be hungry?'

If looks could kill, Keira would have murdered the inventor of the phrase for daring to pass comment on her. Daniel held up his hands in pacification, and she narrowed her eyes.

'Better throw some candy floss in there too.'

Daniel vigorously nodded his agreement.

Outside, they made the short walk from the Wok House towards the cinema, and Daniel had to squint his eyes against the bright white buildings shining in the December sun, the glare enough to spark a slight headache.

As the cinema neared, he felt a tug on his sleeve and looked down, expecting it to be Rosanna, but the five year old had one hand in her pocket and the other in Keira's own. Another tug, and Daniel realised it was coming from behind him. He whirled around, slightly on his guard – you never knew what you were going to meet in town – then stopped short altogether.

It took Keira a moment to realise Daniel was no longer walking alongside them, and when she turned around, he was glued to the spot, unmoving. 'Daniel?'

A homeless man stood before him, or at least, that was the impression he gave off. Shabbily clothed in what appeared to be a decades-old jacket, a threadbare scarf, torn jeans and disintegrating loafers, it wasn't the man's clothes that froze him.

'Please,' the vagrant wheezed, a voice worn by years of smoke and disuse. He held a styrofoam cup in front of him. 'If you have any change…'

Daniel stared at the man's scraggly dark beard, at his slightly hooked nose, at his crooked yellow teeth, but more than any of that, he stared at the man's eyes. Daniel's mouth hung open but he found himself unable to speak, let alone reach for his pockets.

'Daniel,' Keira said, and slipped an arm round his. Daniel barely felt it. 'Come on, let's go.'

He could no more go than he could talk. The bright white paint pierced his eyes like asbestos, and rendered his breathing void.

'Do you have any change, please?' the homeless man said to Keira now, and Daniel stared dumbly as she stuck a hand in her purse and dropped a euro coin into the man's cup.

'Thank you.' The man bowed his head. 'Thank you so much.'

Keira pulled Daniel away as the hobo shuffled off down the street, the only one who'd spoken since seeing the man. Rosanna had watched it all in the same stunned silence of Daniel's own.

'What the hell was that?' Keira asked once they'd put a bit of distance behind them.

'I…' He daren't say it, daren't think it.

'Daniel, are you okay? You've gone incredibly white.'

Daniel swallowed, nodded. 'Fine, fine, I'm good, yeah, fine.' They were almost outside the cinema. 'Can we go home, though?' he asked, and surprised himself at how young he sounded, like a boy asking his mother. Or his grandmother.

Keira stopped and looked at him, then looked down at Rosanna, who held a slight frown at the chance her cinema trip would be cancelled.

'Who was that, Daniel? Do you know that man?'

'Know him?' Daniel found he wasn't looking back at Keira but rather staring at the sky. It was the only way to escape that overpowering, pounding whiteness that pierced the edge of his vision. 'No, no. How could I?'

Keira stopped to squeeze his hand, pulled his face down to meet hers. 'Daniel I've never seen you like this, will you please tell me what's going on? Who was that guy?'

Daniel couldn't bring himself to meet her eyes. 'Let's just get back to the car.'

'What about the cimena?' Rosanna asked.

Keira patted her on the shoulder. 'We can watch a movie when we go home, okay?'

Rosanna's frown became a pout, but she didn't speak up. Keira ruffled her hair, then looked back at Daniel with some concern. She didn't say anything, but let her eyes ask the question.

'The car,' Daniel repeated.

'Okay...' Keira said. 'But it's this way, you know?'

So it was, Daniel realised, and turned on the spot. Why did everything have to be so damned bright? All this bloody paint. He couldn't see and he couldn't think, couldn't *breathe*, and his head hurt like a motherfucker and –

Woah.

Daniel blinked slowly, and looked around. He was in the passenger seat of the car, Keira driving beside him. 'What...?'

'Are you alright?' Keira asked. 'I think you got bloody sunstroke or something. In freaking December. Drink some more water there.'

Daniel saw he held a half-finished water bottle in his hand, swigged from it and was glad he did. 'How... how long was I out?'

'Out? You were asleep?'

Daniel nodded. 'Must have been.'

'Well, you almost fell over getting back into the car, do you remember that?'

Daniel shook his head.

'Jesus.' Keira shot him a worried look. 'You really do need to get out of that fucking attic more.'

Daniel stared out the passenger window at the sea, something he ventured into shockingly little given his proximity to it. As far as he could recall, Granny Cawley had only taken him to Ballyfarreg's shining beach on one or two occasions, but as he stared at it now, he realised he had older memories of sand, ones that pre-dated her.

'Daniel,' Keira said softly, 'will you please tell me now?'

'Tell you what?' Daniel asked, picturing the beard, picturing the teeth.

'You know what.'

Daniel only shook his head.

Keira sighed as they passed the last traffic light on the way out of town.

Daniel envisioned the homeless man's nose, lightly rounded, slightly bent, a bit like his own.

'Please, Daniel,' Keira said, for what he knew would be the last time. 'Who was that?'

Daniel cast a glance at the rear-view mirror, where Rosanna stared out at the sea much like he had, and pictured the homeless man's eyes. Striking blue, exactly like his own.

'I think that was my father.'

15

Keira tried to steer Daniel into the bedroom as soon as they were home but he shrugged her off and made straight for the kitchen, and the album marked *Martin & Helen's Wedding*.

'Daniel…'

Her voice was nothing more than a distant buzz as he stared into his father's youthful face, younger even than Daniel was now, and forever he'd stay that way. Or so Daniel had always thought.

'Look,' he said, handing her the photo. Of course, the tuxedoed man in the picture was nothing like the person they'd seen today. There wasn't a wrinkle in sight, nor the barest hint of that ragged beard. Indeed, his teeth shone brilliant white and his nose was only slightly bent, nothing like that crooked mess in town, but it still held that rounded edge by the nostrils, and those eyes, those eyes were the same.

Keira's own eyes flicked up, down, over and across the photo, never settling. When at last she looked back at Daniel, her face was wracked with concern. 'Daniel –'

'You don't believe me.'

'I just think you're really tired, and –'

'Look at his eyes! They're *my* eyes.'

Keira only looked at him, and when he could take that pitying look no longer, he swiped back the album.

'That was him today. *This* was him. I know it was.'

'You need to rest. Come on, let's go inside and –'

'I don't remember my father's funeral.'

At last, he had her attention.

'What?'

'I remember Mum's, kind of,' Daniel said, in a rush to get it all out, 'I remember the faces at least, and the coffin, and her in it. But I don't remember my dad's. Why is that?'

'I don't know,' Keira said. She eyed him warily. 'It was a traumatic time, maybe you repressed it.'

'How come I remember Mum's then? They would have been at the same time, right?'

Keira didn't answer, looked over her shoulder to check whether Rosanna's room was shut.

'What if he's not dead?' Daniel asked, his eyes wild.

Keira bit her lip, watched him.

'What if he survived the car crash somehow?'

'That… that doesn't make any sense, Daniel.' Her voice was rational, logical, pained. 'If he'd survived the crash then you wouldn't have spent your entire childhood living with your granny.'

'Well what if he…'

'What if he what?'

Daniel swallowed. 'What if he killed her? What if he staged the crash and ran away?'

'And stayed here? In town? Come on Daniel, let this go.'

'Well maybe he did! If he did the rest of it then he clearly wasn't stable. He could have run off, fled the country or something. He might only be back now.'

'Where did the crash happen?'

'I don't know,' Daniel said quickly. 'Why does that matter?'

Keira blinked. 'You don't know?'

'My granny never told me.'

Keira's eyes bulged. 'And you never thought to find out for yourself? Jesus Christ, Daniel, don't you want to know what happened to them?'

Daniel's mouth hung open, and in realising this he snapped it shut. 'I... I always meant to.'

Keira rubbed her forehead. 'How can you... I mean, are you not literally writing a book based on your family's history? How can you not know where your parents died?'

For once, Daniel had no reply.

'Look at me Daniel,' Keira said, and snatched back the album, flicked it open to the first page. '*This* man, this man is your father. This is not the same man we saw in town earlier, thirty years apart or no. There's not even a resemblance.'

'But the eyes –'

'Don't give me that shit about the eyes. Yeah, his eyes were blue. So what? Your eyes are blue, my eyes are blue, Rosanna's are hazel. It doesn't mean a thing.'

Orange, Daniel thought. To him they would always be orange, not hazel.

'Listen to me Daniel,' Keira said, and he did. 'For whatever reason, your dad is on your mind right now. Maybe it's because of what you're writing, you could be digging up old wounds you didn't even know you had, I don't know, but you need to trust me on this. You need rest. That was just some homeless guy we saw today.'

Daniel swallowed hard, not sure if he believed it – sure, if anything, that he didn't – but he nodded all the same.

69

'You need to get closure about your dad,' she said, and Daniel felt the lump in his throat swell. 'Go to the library, look at the local newspaper archives or something. I'm sure a tragedy like that would have made the headlines.'

Daniel's shoulders slumped as he nodded again.

'But not now,' Keira said. 'First you go rest, okay?'

'Okay,' he said, and took the photo off her for one last look before setting it back down on the table. 'I think…' He swallowed, trying to clear the lump. 'I think I might meet Joe later. He texted me earlier asking if I wanted to meet him for a drink or two, maybe that's not such a terrible idea.'

Keira's concern deepened to something approaching a frown, then she sighed. 'Maybe you should, I don't know. You could do with the break. But if you do, don't come back too late. I've work in the morning, remember.'

Daniel did allow himself to be directed into the bedroom then, and more or less as soon as his head hit the pillow, he was out.

*

'Almost didn't expect you to show up,' Joe said and clapped Daniel on the shoulder as he set down the first two pints of the evening. 'What with the whole waiting four hours to reply shtick.'

Daniel eyed the frosty yellow liquid sceptically. 'What is that, Tuborg? You're fairly stretching the aul purse strings there.'

'Well excuse me, didn't realise I was dining with royalty. The queen give you your MBE yet?'

'Ah feck off,' Daniel said, and sipped. 'Wow.'

'Damn bloody right wow, and don't you go doubting these purse strings again. Those at the bottom of the bag are often the richest in character.'

'That how you'd describe yourself, is it?'

'Now you feck off,' Joe said as his eyes tracked the swishing skirt of some young one on her way to the bathroom.

'You got a client for that?'

Joe's head flicked back, eyebrows raised. 'For what?'

'For all that rubber in your neck. You stand to make a pretty penny.'

'Ah g'way you. Sure don't I have a woman these days?'

Now here was news. 'Oh yeah?' Daniel asked. 'Not like you to meet someone, and then continue to meet them.'

'I can carry a relationship if needs be.'

'Can you now? I've yet to see it done. So who's the unlucky lady?'

'Ah, leave it out with that,' Joe said, and, to Daniel's utter astonishment, looked away sheepishly.

'What?' Daniel asked, leaning forward. 'Who is it?'

Joe's eyes scanned the pub, as if anyone gave a damn. 'Don't laugh.'

'Don't –' Daniel leant further in so that their noses practically touched. 'Does she have a reputation or something?'

'No, no, nothing like that. It's just… Jesus Christ, me and my mouth, I shouldn't have said anything. Forget I said anything.'

'Well I'm hardly going to forget about it now, am I? Just tell me man!'

Joe gulped the pint till it was half-gone. 'Promise you won't make fun?'

'Like blood from a fucking stone you are,' Daniel said, but when that didn't budge him, 'Fine, fine, I promise I won't make fun. Well, not unless I really have to.'

Joe sighed. 'I guess that'll have to do.' He drank, swashed it around in his mouth, swallowed, then sighed again. 'It's Caitlyn.'

'Caitlyn?' Daniel furrowed his brows. 'Caitlyn…' His eyes widened. 'Caitlyn *Moran*?' he almost yelled, and Joe shrank away under his voice. 'Jesus Christ Joe, she's your…' Joe's eyes made Daniel catch himself right before he finished as numerous heads actually did swing their way. He waited for them to turn back, then leaned in again and lowered his voice. 'Is she not your fucking cousin Joe?'

Joe shook his head quickly, too quickly for Daniel's liking. 'Half-cousin,' he said. 'She's adopted.'

Daniel knew Caitlyn from primary school, before she and her family – Joe's family! – moved to Wicklow, a long time back now, but he soon conjured up a loose picture of her in his head. Light brown hair, short of figure, dark eyes. Essentially Joe, if he were a woman. 'She looks like your twin, man!'

'Yeah, well, she isn't. I've known that since we were twelve and she wouldn't take her hands off me all summer.'

72

'Bullshit.' Daniel clearly remembered that summer as the one he and Joe had spent the entirety of in the latter's back garden, trying and failing to build a treehouse as their last hurrah before secondary school. 'Where was I in all of this?'

'Okay, well maybe not *all* summer,' Joe said, 'but every time Mum took me to her house.'

'To your mum's sister's house,' Daniel said, and Joe waved him away with the flick of a wrist.

'I knew I shouldn't have told you,' he said, and downed the last of his pint before rising from his seat.

'Will you hang on a second?' Daniel grabbed a hold of his arm and pulled him back down.

Joe sat sullenly with his arms folded. 'What?'

'Listen...' Daniel rubbed his forehead. Listen to what? A lecture on how incest was wrong, perhaps? When he didn't continue, Joe made to get up from again and Daniel held up a hand. 'Alright, look. Forgive my reaction, but you can probably understand where I was coming from.' Joe didn't nod, but nor did he disagree. Daniel kept going. 'I'm sure you know well enough for yourself who your relatives are, so why don't you tell me a little bit about her, other than the fact that the two of ye aren't cousins?'

'Well we are *half*-cousins...' Joe said, and the side of his mouth twisted into a grin.

'That turn you on does it? Can't say I'm surprised.'

'Sick bastard.'

73

'Nah, that'll be your children,' Daniel said, and before Joe could answer, quickly shot up from his seat. 'Next round's on me. And if your sister walks by, try and keep your hands to yourself.'

Joe's cursed reply was muted by the hustle and bustle of Kelleher's pub, the lifeblood of good old seaside Ballyfarreg, and the pair's stomping ground of years gone by. As Daniel let the ridiculousness of Joe's revelation wash over him, and the pissy lager wash out of him, he couldn't but be a little nostalgic for it all. He and Joe, out again, downing pints, banging cousins, hon the lads.

He returned with the next round as Joe eloquently defended his reasoning.

'I mean, if you had a hot cousin, and then it turned out she wasn't your cousin, wouldn't you bang her?'

'Well, personally I would maybe just consider for a moment the fallout such a thing would cause –'

'Lies, lies, I can see it in your eyes! Big titty Jacintha comes up from Limerick and plonks herself down in your lap, says Uncle Mick doesn't quite give it like he used to –'

'Jesus Christ.'

'– and she's staring up at you, smiling with those big pearly whites, eyes practically screaming "Fuck me! Fuck me!" and *you're* saying you wouldn't –'

'Alright, knock it off,' Daniel said, and meant it too. All that talk of eyes… he didn't want to think about that right now.

Joe must have sensed the mirth gone out of his voice. 'Well, enough about me anyway, it's not like you'd understand, cousinless as you are. How's life treating my second favourite regionally-based writer?'

Daniel grunted. 'Still chipping away at Amy then?'

'Eh, I wouldn't say that. I have my big titty Jacintha, after all. That is, unless you think she'd be up for a –'

'Pretty sure she's just gay, Joe.'

'Really? After that time with you and Keira I thought –'

'Leave it out, yeah?'

'Right, right, sorry. Only messing with you.'

'I know you are.' Daniel sighed, offered a weak smile. 'Don't worry about it, I've just got some things on my plate right now.'

'Yeah?'

'Yeah.'

'Well if I can trouble you for another round, can you trouble me to tell them?'

Daniel looked at Joe but in his mind's eye saw only his father. He nodded. 'Go on then.'

Joe returned moments later with not two, but four pints of Guinness. 'That should tide us over.'

Daniel couldn't help smiling. 'Just how fucked up do you think I am?'

'Well see, where you've a talent for writing stories, I've a talent for knowing how much drink is necessary to get through them.' He handed Daniel one of the pints. 'Speaking of, and before you begin, how is the writing going? I'm halfway through *Fire Flies* and want to know how long I've to wait for the next one.'

'Seeing as that's been out about four years Joe, I can't imagine you've too much to worry about.'

'Ah yeah, but how's it going anyways? I can tell you're dying to talk about it.'

'It's going good, I guess,' Daniel said. 'Sticking to a fairly regular morning schedule so that I can get the work done while the women are away and I've the house to myself. Sometimes that'll carry over into the weekend, depending on how I'm feeling.'

'Get much done today?'

'Yeah, I...' wait, had he? Daniel paused. Today, what day was today? Sunday. Certainly, he'd gone up to the attic this morning, that's when he'd found the broken pint glass after all, but had he written anything? Surely he must have, because that had been very early, and by the time he'd come downstairs for breakfast, Keira was already asking him about lunch. 'Huh.'

'Something up?'

'No, nothing.' But it wasn't nothing. Why couldn't he remember if he'd written anything?

'Daniel?' Joe's voice crept in from very far away. 'Are you alright man?'

Daniel's head had started to spin, and once it started, there was no stopping it. On it spun, to the point he couldn't speak, and so he nodded instead, which only made it worse. His clothes felt damp and sticky against his person, and he realised he was sweating.

'Jesus, Daniel, are you okay? You look like you're going to be –'

Daniel staggered out of his chair, hands over mouth as he stumbled towards the bathroom, the whole pub spinning, a mix of lights and laughter and that swishing skirt again, faces and noises and none of them natural, none of them human, and the wooden door swung inward and at last Daniel was faced with the cold clarity of the tavern toilet.

His face barely made it over the bowl before he was heaving, chunks of spice bag, prawn curry and creamy milk stout forming a vile concoction as they rose in his throat and made soup of the water. As he heaved, he choked too, and coughed, and spluttered, and suddenly he realised that it wasn't a simple choke, he was actually *choking*. Fear ripped through him as he gagged and he spat, no air coming in, no air going out, sweat coursing in rivulets as he shook his head and reached for his throat praying all the while not here, please God not here, not in the bathroom of Kelleher's pub, the same fucking stall where he'd gotten his first handjob off Jodie Fitzsimmons in what would literally be another lifetime ago, please God not –

The thing lodged in his throat came loose and expunged itself, the texture so revoltingly fuzzy and foreign to the human oesophagus that he very nearly threw up again, until he saw what it was he'd expelled and had the wind knocked so clean out of him that he couldn't have even done that.

Staring back up at him from the revolting broth of his stomach's brew, like some horrid hairball grinning at an indignified cat, about the size of a tennis ball, was a patch of putrid green moss.

14

Daniel shivered as he traded the cold street air for the library's dusty interior. It was busy enough, far more than he'd expected for a Monday afternoon, which served to make his cold sweating all the more noticeable. He wanted to get this done and over with, before things slipped even further out of his control.

A middle-aged black woman with short brown hair and glasses sat behind the main desk, and Daniel approached with what he hoped was a friendly smile, and not the wheedling junkie's grin he feared it to be.

'Hiya,' he said, too loudly, and at the librarian's wince, lowered his voice. 'I'm looking for the newspaper archives, do you keep them here?'

The librarian nodded, her voice about fifty decibels shy of his own. 'Do you know what newspaper you're looking for?'

'The *Herald*, preferably.'

The librarian hacked something into her keyboard. 'Did you have a specific date in mind?'

Daniel pursed his lips. His parents had died on the 26th of May 1987, but if the paper released in bi-weekly instalments then as it did today, there was no telling when the first mention of the accident would be. 'Anything from the end of May through June 1987.'

The librarian clicked her mouse and nodded. 'I have six papers from May the 24th to Tuesday the 11th, will that do?'

'Yes, perfect.'

'We have them in hard copy or microfilm, which would you prefer?'

'Microfilm,' Daniel said after another short pause. He'd learned how to use it in college and some strange nostalgia bell had just dinged in his head commanding him to choose it.

'Do you need any help setting up?'

'No, no thank you.'

'Give me a moment then and I'll go fetch them.'

Daniel thanked the woman and waited patiently until she returned with the reels, one for May and one for June, and followed in silence as she led him to the scanner. Two minutes with the dinosaur of a machine and Daniel regretted his decision not to go for the simple hardcopy. If it wasn't bad enough that he couldn't remember which way the reel went in, then it was even worse that he'd completely forgotten which buttons needed pressing. Finally, after what felt like an hour but was probably only ten minutes of jigging and re-working, he had the May reel up and running.

Daniel scrolled straight to the end of the month, past the Sunday the 24th edition and onto Thursday the 28th's, where he was greeted by a headline that stopped his heart.

TRAGEDY AT BALLYFARREG – MOTHER OF ONE KILLED, FATHER MISSING IN FATAL CAR ACCIDENT ON OLD FAMINE ROAD

Daniel's tongue went completely dry as he scanned the headline once, twice, three times. He shook his head, and when that didn't feel like enough, shook it again. He couldn't… what? *What*? Father missing? Old famine road? What??

Daniel tried to still his thumping heart, couldn't. He blinked, hoping it would somehow alter the headline. It didn't. His breath came weakly, didn't come at all. The famine road? *His* famine road? The headline confirmed it. Ballyfarreg. How many other famine roads could there be in the vicinity? That was his road, those were his parents. But how? *Father missing*? How?

With nothing else for it, Daniel read on. The words, plain English, the same he'd read all his life, made no sense to him.

Thirty-three year-old Martin Cawley, father of one, remains missing following a tragic car accident on an old famine road in lower Ballyfarreg. His wife, twenty-nine year-old Helen Cawley, was pronounced dead at the scene at 3pm, Tuesday afternoon. Gardaí say that substantial blood loss on the driver's side of the vehicle, where Mr. Cawley was thrust through the windshield after colliding with a tree to the side of the heavily forested road, mean there is little chance of his survival. They believe that, following the crash and the blood loss,

Cawley may have become delirious and wandered off into the forest, where the search for his body continues.

What were they doing there? Daniel's head swelled, pulsed, pounded. He wanted to scream, cry, punch. The road didn't even go anywhere!

There was more, and Daniel read on in a state of shock, thirty years' worth of suppressed emotion coming to the fore all at once. How had he let Keira talk him into this? How had he thought it would be a good idea? Why hadn't his granny ever told him? What the hell were they doing there?

It was initially believed that Martin and Helen Cawley had been visiting Martin's mother, Marie Cawley, who resides in lower Ballyfarreg, shortly before the crash occurred, but following an interview with Mrs. Cawley, she revealed that the two had not been to her house that day. In fact, Mrs. Cawley said during the interview that it had been over a year since she'd seen either her son or daughter-in-law, and when the interviewer brought up the topic of their being on the famine road, and the failure to recover Mr. Cawley's body thus far, she refused to answer any further questions.

Gardaí are baffled by the reasoning behind the crash, and they will be unable to determine its cause until Mr. Cawley's body is found, they say. An autopsy will be carried out on Helen Cawley's body in order to shed any light it can on the case, but for now, the mystery behind this one continues.

And that was it. That was the whole article. No mention of him, apart from his existence as the child of a mother and father of one, and nothing to answer any of the many, many, burning questions within him. Like, if the Gardaí were so certain of his father's death, then how bad must the crash have been? Why couldn't they determine the cause until his body was found? Did they think he was drinking? *Had* he been drinking? Why had his granny refused to answer any more questions? *What the hell were they doing there?* And where, oh where, was his father's body?

The sound of footsteps approaching, and Daniel very nearly jumped out of his seat. He whipped around and saw that it was just the librarian again, come to check how he was getting on with the microfilm. She must have seen the look on his face because she quickly backed off, and despite Daniel's assurances that everything was fine, hesitated a moment longer before returning to where she'd come.

The brief encounter having somewhat returned Daniel to reality, he checked his phone and saw that it was 1.54pm.

'Shit!' he hissed.

Rosanna would be finished any minute now, but he was far from done. Far, far from done. Still, he could hardly stay and leave her stuck in limbo at school, so with a thunderous heart he hit print on the remaining pages in the May reel, then went ahead and did the same for all of June. He'd go through them later once he was home.

The total for printing the pages came to six euro and forty-seven cents, a charge Daniel forgot he'd have to pay until he returned the reels and the librarian saw his many sheets of paper. He gave her a tenner and told her to keep the rest, thinking that in doing so it might encourage her to keep her mouth shut about the frantic sweaty man she'd seen in the library today, but after he saw her pocket the change he realised that if anything it would only add to her story. He brushed this aside – what choice did he have? – thanked her again, then dipped out of the library, hopped into his car, and sped off to collect Rosanna.

*

Daniel had just gotten Rosanna into her seatbelt when a text from Keira totally disrupted his plans for the day.

Hey, just got a call from Mum there. She and Dad are down for a surprise visit and they're at the house already but she says no-one's home, I assume you're with Rosanna?? Anyways, I wish she would have texted me or something but they're both there now and have let themselves in. Did you not lock the door when you left?? You should be more careful. Sorry, this is turning into a rant. Just hurry home and try keep them entertained until I'm finished. Love youuuu xxxx

'Fuck,' Daniel said aloud, and got a frown from an old woman passing by, which only deepened when she saw Rosanna within earshot. Daniel grimaced and sidled round to the driver's door, trying to put some order on his roiling thoughts.

If Stephen and Mary were down from Meath, then there was no way he was going to be able to read the rest of the madness anytime soon. Unless he read it now of course. But did he really want to do that with Rosanna sitting right behind him in the back seat? Daniel looked at her in the rear-view mirror, watched her stare placidly back at him. Cold fingers ran over him, a bad omen. He shook his head and started the car. The papers would have to wait. He would have to wait. Just until Keira got home. That was doable, right?

Daniel found he still hadn't taken his eyes off Rosanna, nor she off him. *What are you looking at?* came the bizarre demand from somewhere within him. Almost as if he'd said it out loud, Rosanna tilted her head, and for a minute, Daniel wondered if he hadn't said it out loud, but the next thing he knew the car was inching forward onto the road away from the primary school and he had to quickly switch gears both mentally and physically before he let reality slip away entirely.

'Everything alright back there, Rosie?'

'Yeah,' she said simply, and turned her attention out the window.

My father is dead, Daniel assured himself as the village fell away behind them. He knew this. He'd been dead for thirty years. This he also knew. Only that wasn't what the *Herald* said, was it? *Mother* of one dead, that was what the paper had said. Father *missing*. Missing, presumed dead. Presumed. Daniel couldn't help but keep his gaze from flicking back and forth from the road to the stack of printed sheets in the passenger seat beside him.

Fucking Stephen and Mary. Fucking Keira. Why couldn't her parents have died in ridiculous circumstances? Why couldn't it be his parents down for a surprise visit on a freezing December afternoon, of all the fucking times? Then again Daniel had to be careful what he wished for – his father may still only be "missing" after all. He barked a short, mad laugh at this, and winced at Rosanna's appraising look in the mirror.

He was in for a long day.

*

'She's gotten so big, hasn't she?' Mary crooned over her grand-daughter from the living room couch where she and Stephen sat, as the child showed her grandmother her sketchpad. Daniel stood by the kitchen counter making tea. 'Though I suppose you tend not to notice it.'

Daniel shrugged, unsure of whether or not this was some sort of dig. Rosanna smiled at the "big" comment, and ran off to her room to get some more drawings to show Mary. There was little doubt in his mind that Keira's parents would much prefer that she and him live somewhere closer to what they knew as home. Every time they visited there would be some off-hand comment like this one, innocent enough so that Daniel couldn't tell if he was imagining things, but loaded with just the right amount of guilt-tripping to make him believe they saw him as robbing the pair of a grandchild.

Or, even worse, depriving Rosanna of her grandparents. *I had a grandparent*, he thought, picturing the crash again, so close to this very home. *Some good it did me.*

'She's about right for her age,' he said as he brought over the tea. 'A bit on the short side, if anything.'

'Oh I'm sure, I'm sure. It's just been so long,' Mary said as she accepted the mug with a smile. Stephen grunted his appreciation, though he eyed the contents of the mug somewhat sceptically. 'So, is there anything exciting going on in this part of the world?' Mary asked, as if it wasn't a paltry two hour drive from home.

Well, my father may not actually be dead and I threw up a glob of moss last night, my whole body feels like it's being drained of blood a millilitre at a time and there's the slight chance that I'm going insane, but apart from that, no, nothing much.

'Not really,' Daniel said. 'Except for the cold, it seems a lot harsher than usual.'

'Ha!' Stephen laughed, deigning to speak for the first time since they'd exchanged greetings. 'You'd better get used to that.'

Mary threw him a sideways glance, then nodded at Daniel. 'I know what you mean, it dropped eight degrees on the way over here.'

Daniel whistled, not out of surprise, but because it required less effort than an actual response. Conversation didn't suit him right now, all he could think of was the stack of printed papers on his passenger seat.

'Aren't you going to sit down?' Mary asked, and Daniel realised he'd just been standing in the middle of the room after handing over their drinks. He turned his head to hide the flush that threatened to rise in his cheeks and sat on the armchair opposite the two.

The moment he sat down, Rosanna came bounding back into the room with two more sketchpads and promptly sat herself between Stephen and Mary.

'What do you have there?' Stephen asked, but Rosanna only smiled shyly as she opened the pad to reveal her first doodles.

Mary leaned across to Daniel and spoke in a hushed tone. 'She still isn't very talkative, is she?'

Not towards strangers, Daniel thought, but knew better than to say it aloud. He gave Mary a polite smile and tried to think how best to answer this, but the words that came out surprised him. 'So how long are you planning on staying for?' His light tone was just enough to stop the question from coming across as what, at its heart, it was. Rude.

'Oh, we're not sure yet,' Mary said, 'We thought we might head to the beach at some point, it's so much prettier in winter, wouldn't you say? Only I think we might have left it a bit late for today.'

Daniel resisted the urge to grimace. A bit late for today, but what about tomorrow? 'So, you'll stay until dinner then?'

Mary turned to Stephen and vice versa, as if they hadn't already decided on this themselves before setting out this morning.

'Well, if that's okay with you and Keira,' Mary said, but it didn't come across as a question.

'Of course, that'd be perfect,' Daniel said, and offered them his most winning smile, widening it again when they smiled back. He wondered who out of the three of them was the best at faking it. Not Stephen, anyway.

'What time does Keira usually get back?' her father asked, staring at the wall-clock with even more intensity than Daniel, the look of a man who could only look at a Junior Infant's scribbles for so long.

'Quarter-past four, in around,' Daniel said, a little under ninety minutes away.

Stephen nodded and Mary smiled, slightly less enthusiastic this time. As the silence stretched on, the newspaper headline flashed through his mind again, and Daniel had to stop himself from asking them why they'd come so damn early.

'Did you hear the news about Amy?' he asked, not sure why, just knowing he had to say *something* to make the passage of time at least bearable.

Mary's eyes lit up at the mention of the name. 'No, what happened there?'

Daniel paused. Did Mary know? About Keira and... surely not. Why the hell had he brought her up? As if his mood wasn't bad enough. 'Her book's being made into a film.'

'Oh, brilliant!' Mary said, and she gave her husband's arm a tug, pulling him away from Rosanna's drawings. 'Did you hear that Stephen?'

'Hear what?'

'Amy's book is being turned into a film.'

'Oh right,' Stephen said, and gave Daniel a look. Sympathy, or disappointment? 'Good for her,' his father-in-law continued, 'I've always liked Amy. Lovely girl.'

Daniel nodded, the blood that wasn't being drained out of him boiling. Stephen and Mary both seemed to be staring at him, as if they were waiting for a glowing endorsement of Amy from himself.

'She's an incredibly talented writer,' he said, and the pair smiled at him again. Compliment paid, Daniel looked at the clock. Eighty-six minutes to go.

*

Try as he might, Daniel could never work for himself an opportunity to slip out to his car unnoticed, even after Keira got home. The fact that it should have been such a simple, banal thing, not at all worthy of mention, made it all the more difficult for him. If he loudly proclaimed that he was going out to the car, then they'd wonder what he might be doing for it to be such a big deal. If he went without a word, they might wonder where he'd gone off to, and come looking for him. And even if he did manage to escape unseen for a few minutes, just long enough to get the whole story straight in his mind, what if it unsettled him further, rather than putting things right? It was all too much and he too little, and the next thing he knew, mashed potatoes were being passed across the kitchen table in front of him, and the stack of newspapers were still very much in his car.

'So, was he a good host while I was out?' Keira asked.

Stephen merely raised an eyebrow at the question so focused was he on his spuds, but Mary nodded her head vehemently. 'Oh yes, he told us all about Amy's movie.' The smile that lit her face didn't look faked then.

'Did he now?' Keira asked, and gave Daniel a sidelong glance. He thought he saw her own smile slip, just a little. 'And what did he have to say?'

'He said they might be filming some of it down by the beach there, come the new year. Isn't that just fantastic?'

Daniel let the words wash over him as he turned his attention to Rosanna beside him, playing with her salmon. She sliced through the centre of the cutlet with her knife, and used the fork to bury the basil Keira had used as garnish deep inside the slit, then went about with her veg as if nothing had happened.

'Aren't you going to eat your salmon, Rosie?'

Rosanna shook her head. 'Don't eat fish. It makes me sad for Spot.'

Daniel's eyes flicked to their motionless pet, transfixed by his own reflection. 'I don't think he'll particularly mind.'

The child shrugged. 'I mind.'

'Well looky here, do we have a little vegan on our hands?' Mary asked. 'How adorable.'

Keira and Daniel shared a look, but neither deigned to share that Rosanna's favourite meal was unequivocally a barbecue burger.

'So Daniel,' Stephen began, completely oblivious of how much he was about to shatter the ambiance of the room. 'Keira tells us you think you saw your father yesterday?'

He said it between a forkful of carrots and mashed potatoes, and didn't seem to notice as both Keira and Mary's mouths dropped open, and stared at him with wide eyes.

Daniel felt as if he'd been punched, and his own mouth hung open as he looked to Keira, who held his gaze for only a second before she was unable to face the look in his eyes. Mary gawped at her husband with utter disbelief, but Stephen, who hadn't sensed a thing, continued.

'Do you have a history of mental illness in your family, Daniel?'

'Stephen!'

'Dad!'

Daniel could only stare at the old man, slack-jawed, as his fingers clenched round knife and fork. Slowly, he chewed the food in his mouth, and swallowed. 'Well I wouldn't know, would I?'

Stephen laughed briefly – 'Ha!' – thinking Daniel was making some sort of quip, then quickly turned it into a cough when he saw the look on his face. 'Oh, pardon me, I meant no offence, it's just an odd thing to think, isn't it? I know if I saw my father after thirty years I'd head straight for the hills.'

Keira implored Daniel, a pained look on her face, but he refused to meet her eyes, instead turned them upon his food. Was that why they were here, Stephen and Mary? Had Keira rang them up last night and told them to come down while he was out with Joe? Daniel could feel the hair on his arms and neck bristle as he considered the possibilities. A surprise visit, out of the blue, during school time? How could he have been so stupid as to believe a story like that?

'Daniel's been very stressed lately,' Keira said quickly. 'Overworked, I mean. He just needs to get out of the house more. Clear his head.'

Mary nodded rapidly, coming quick to her daughter's aid. 'I think we could all do with some of that. Why don't you come along with us to the beach tomorrow, Daniel?'

'No thank you,' Daniel said. Even to himself, his voice sounded mechanical. 'I'm behind on my writing.'

'Ah, one day can't hurt, can it?' Stephen asked, throwing back another forkful of mash.

'More than you'd think,' he said through gritted teeth.

The quartet returned to their food, and the topic of Daniel's father and mental illness did not come up again. From the corner of his vision – he would not look at her – Keira eyed him worriedly.

That night, as he finished setting up Rosanna's room with an inflatable mattress for Keira, and Stephen and Mary got settled in his own, she came in to see how he was doing.

'Daniel I–'

'Don't,' he said. 'Just don't. I'm sleeping on the couch.'

Keira tried to stop him from leaving the room, her lip trembling as she did so, but he barged past her without looking back, and she didn't follow. Good. He needed to be alone.

Lying on the couch then, he tried not to think at all, about anything. Not about Keira, or her parents, or his own. If he wanted, he could go out to the car and get the newspaper now, but for whatever reason – for so many reasons – he no longer wanted to. He was so utterly demoralised and exhausted, so sick of thinking and processing, and he just didn't believe that anything good would come of it. He allowed himself to drift off without so much as a cushion under his head.

13

A loud bang from the hallway snapped Daniel's eyes open. He groaned as he rose, every muscle stiff from hours on the couch, and his eyes found the clock on the wall, barely visible in the darkness, which told him it was 2.15am. Who the hell was banging on the door at this hour?

Daniel rolled off the couch and into the grey light of the hallway, illumined through the door's frosted window. Another loud bang, and it shook in its frame. Daniel stopped where he was, halfway down the hall, rubbed his eyes. Had he imagined that, or had he seen it?

It came again, the door shook again, and Daniel's skin prickled. His eyes flicked to Rosanna's room, so close to the entrance, his tongue dry. How were she and Keira sleeping through this?

Timidly, he put another step forward, and the door banged again. And again. And again. It kept banging, each strike rattling not only the door but the floor and the walls too. The strikes quickened in tandem with the frantic beating of Daniel's chest.

Thud-thud-thud, went his heart.

BANG-BANG-BANG, went the door.

Thud-BANG-Thud-BANG-Thud-BANG.

What the hell was happening? Who was out there? Why was he the only one hearing it? Daniel felt a wave of nausea threaten to overcome him and swallowed it down.

Suddenly, the banging stopped, and Daniel allowed himself to breathe for a second, but it was quickly replaced by a scratching sound, a scuffling. *The flowerpot.* Daniel stood dumbly in the middle of the hall. There was a spare key under the flowerpot.

God knew why he kept it there, it was the first place anyone would look, but Granny Cawley had done it, and old habits died hard. The scraping stopped, and Daniel stumbled backwards as an outline appeared in the door's window.

Keira! I have to help Keira!

But he didn't move, his feet were glued to the spot. Metal clicked, the lock came undone, and the front door swung slowly open. It brought with it the cold night air, icy lips upon his sweating flesh, came all the way ajar, and Daniel watched agonised, paralysed, as the figure stepped inside.

His heart almost fell apart with relief.

Stephen gave a quick start upon seeing him, then held his hands up apologetically from within his robe. 'Ah, Daniel, I'm sorry, didn't mean to wake you. Went out for a smoke and the blasted door locked behind me. Sorry for the noise, I forgot about the key.'

Didn't mean to wake him? He was lucky he hadn't brought the bloody house down! 'Maybe you shouldn't knock so loudly at this hour,' Daniel grated.

'Did I?' Stephen asked, forehead creasing. 'No, no, I only gave it a little rap. Then I remembered the key.'

Daniel thought about the banging, the ear-bursting, house-shaking, earth-shattering banging, and could only shake his head. He turned to go back to the couch when Stephen caught his arm.

'Er, Daniel, listen, about earlier, you have to know I didn't mean anything by it...' he stopped, unable to meet Daniel's eye, and sighed. When he looked up, there was genuine remorse on his weathered face. 'Daniel, my father took his life when I was nineteen.'

Daniel didn't know how to respond. Keira had never told him this.

'He was a… a troubled man, shall we say, and he could never… never talk to anyone about what was going on inside him. Mum left when I was only six, you see, and, well, he never really got over that, but he grit and bore it until I was old enough for college and sent me on my way with a smile and a handshake.' Stephen's voice had lost all manner of the gruffness it held earlier. 'I found out through a letter, one he sent me himself. He didn't explain it, just said he was sorry. That it wasn't my fault. And like that, I was alone.' He smiled sadly at Daniel. 'You have to know when I asked you that earlier that I was coming from a good place. Even if you don't want to hear this, I'll tell you anyways. There are people out there who love you, Daniel, my daughter most of all. And there's always someone you can talk to, always. I just wish I'd told my own father that.'

With that, Stephen clapped him on the shoulder, and disappeared back into the bedroom, without waiting for a reply. Daniel stood in stunned silence, and when he eventually found himself moving again, it was towards Rosanna's room and not the kitchen.

He watched with a tired smile as mother and daughter slept in the child's bed, the air mattress he'd spent so long blowing up left unused. Be a shame to put all that effort to waste.

Keira's cheek was warm as he planted a kiss on her sleeping face, Rosanna's soft as he did the same. He couldn't remember the last time he'd kissed her. Watching her doze like that in her mother's arms, away from the harsh unblinking gaze of her eyes, Daniel wondered what it was that had been holding him back.

As he settled under the blanket on the inflatable mattress, he knew one thing was for certain. It sure as hell beat the couch.

*

The next morning, Keira and Rosanna were both gone by the time he woke up. How they'd slipped out without stirring him, he didn't know, but he was grateful all the same. The events of the previous day had exhausted him, and he'd needed that sleep more than he'd realised.

The sound of a car starting in the driveway alerted him, however, and he looked out the window to see Stephen and Mary in their car, backing up onto the road. It seemed the whole house was content to leave him lie.

Not bothering to get changed, Daniel raced out of the house in his bare feet to bid them farewell.

'Decided to join us after all?' Mary asked, lowering the passenger window.

Daniel smiled. 'No, sorry, duty calls. I just came to say goodbye. It wouldn't do to sleep through your exit now would it?' He looked over to Stephen, behind the wheel. 'And thank you for what you said, it meant a lot.'

Stephen blinked at him. 'What I said?'

Daniel tilted his head. 'Last night, about your father.'

'My father?' Stephen's eyebrows furrowed, thick angry caterpillars. 'I thought it was your father we were talking about.'

Daniel swallowed, his mouth suddenly stale. He looked at Mary, who stared back just as quizzically as her husband. Daniel felt his blood pump in his ears as they watched him, the cool outdoor air growing thinner.

'Y-yes,' he stammered, 'that's what I meant. My father.' Daniel's fingers twitched. He was very hot and very cold all at the same time.

'Okay…' Stephen said. 'You're welcome, I suppose.'

Mary smiled her winning, ingratiating smile again, and Daniel found himself returning the same, though it must have been a crazed attempt, for hers started to slip. 'Well we really should be going,' she said, 'thank you for being such a lovely host.'

Daniel nodded. He couldn't speak. Couldn't breathe. He watched in aching silence as the two drove off, and, once they were out of sight, turned and sprinted back towards the house, not caring for the pebbles that dug at his soles.

My father? I thought it was your father we were talking about.

The banging.

Thud-BANG-Thud-BANG-Thud-BANG.

'No, no, I only gave it a little rap.'

'Oh my Christ,' Daniel moaned. His whole body shook, threatened to give way as he leaned over the bathroom sink. The idea of being sick again so soon made him gag, the irony far from lost on him.

How could he not remember? How could Stephen not remember?

Because that wasn't Stephen.

As soon as the thought came, Daniel knew it was true. Bile rose in his throat and, thankfully, didn't lodge there as he spewed into the sink, every last ounce of his supposed sanity pouring out with it.

How? How and why? How and why and who?

Daniel stared at the haggard shell of himself in the mirror, vomit-stained, pale and scruffy, like he hadn't seen light in years. The urge to scream built in him and he held it back, bit down fiercely on his tongue, hard enough to draw blood, stared at his reflection as red rivulets ran down his chin.

A noise, then, and if it hadn't been for the fact that he was staring at the mirror so intently, if he hadn't watched his mouth open and his jaw extend as the roar escaped him, he wouldn't have known where it had come from. The sound filled his ears as he stared at this face, his face, and it rose to a tremendous, cracking point before eking to a croak, as all the while Daniel watched, mouth open, until silence finally restored.

Then the man in the mirror winked.

Daniel froze.

Had he done that?

He stared at himself, the taste of iron rank on his tongue as he waited for it to happen again. It didn't.

But it had.

Had he winked? Or had his reflection winked at him? Another soft moan escaped him, and he fell back from the sink, away from the bathroom, out into the hallway. He couldn't take this anymore.

His keys sat where he left them in the bowl on the hallway table. His heart thundered as he picked them up, finally alone. So why did he feel so watched?

'And like that, I was alone.'

Stephen had said that. Except, he hadn't. That didn't matter. Daniel needed to put it as far from his brain as he could, the only thing that mattered now was reading the newspaper, finding out what happened to his dad, finding out what happened to Stephen's dad, what happened to Stephen, who was Stephen –

Daniel's mind rolled relentlessly on as he stepped back outside, still in his underwear. So scattered was his brain that he didn't notice the bitter wind lapping at his pale exposed legs. Maybe if he had, things would have been different. As it was, he raced to the passenger side door, ignoring once again the stones that cut into his feet, the hard sting that surely signalled the drawing of blood, he ignored it all, pushed it all to the side as he swung open the car door, and just as he did so, a huge gust of wind roared by, and Daniel watched in stunned horror as its chilling fingers reached into his car, plucked the sheets out from the seat, and sent them sprawling to all four corners of the world.

12

The librarian glanced up and quickly down again at Daniel's approach, suddenly fascinated by the contents of her keyboard.

'Hi, again,' Daniel said, sure to whisper this time, but his conscientiousness was soon offset by a hacking couch.

'Hello,' the woman said, barely suppressing a wince.

'I want the same as yesterday. The *Herald*. May through June nineteen-'

'Yes, I remember. Microfilm again?'

'Sure,' Daniel said, throat tight. 'Or hardcopy, if it's quicker. Whatever's quicker.'

The librarian eyed him askance, but gave a short nod. 'I'll check the back.'

As she disappeared beyond, Daniel leaned up against the counter, sagged. He felt terrible, legs weak, arms heavy, breath a damnable hassle. Flu, probably. Hopefully.

The librarian came back either seconds or hours later with a cardboard box in her hands and a look of bewilderment on her face. 'I just don't know what could have happened to them...'

Daniel stared unblinking down at the sodden mess in front of him, labelled *Herald 1987* in black marker, as she lifted the tattered lid to reveal a mishmash of soggy pink paper, running ink, and weeks upon months of lost information. Now was the part where he screamed.

Only he didn't scream, rather swallowed, sucking back shards of glass as he did so, and politely enquired, 'Maybe the microfilm, then?'

Sat in front of the scanner again, Daniel tried not to let his shaky hands deter him. In the small of his back, he could feel the librarian's gaze on him, and threw a glance over his shoulder, just in time to see her vanish round the corner.

'Okay,' Daniel muttered, the machine finally flitting to life as the same headline as yesterday lit the screen in front of him. 'Here we go.'

If the initial article was the 28th of May then surely he need only scroll onto the June section and... the room grew closer the further he scrolled, he could feel it tighten around his shoulders as the fine print of newspaper pages became tainted by a dark mar at the edges, which thickened page-on-page until it met in the centre, to the point that, rather than staring at a headline entitled June 1st 1987, Daniel stared only at an entirely black screen, and his own reflection in it.

He stood up before it could wink, didn't bother to eject the film, it was corrupted anyway, they were all corrupted, he knew that now, he finally understood, and as he strode straight for the exit, his head awhirl and his stomach aswarm, he had absolutely no idea what he was going to do next.

Back in the car, his knuckles ghostly white in their vice on the wheel, Daniel hung his head, gasping, and tried not to think about anything at all.

*

Daniel sat at the kitchen table, warming his hands round a mug of tea, and stared at the kitchen clock. He had to talk to someone, *burned* to talk to someone, but he couldn't, not for another two hours at least, and even then, that would only be Rosanna. It would be another three on top of that until Keira was home. What the hell did he normally do with so much time?

That he was sick was no longer in any doubt. Once he'd finally worked up the nerve to re-enter the bathroom and look in the mirror, it was like glaring at death made flesh. He hadn't eaten since dinner last night, and even then he'd barely touched it after Stephen's comment – don't think about Stephen – and he certainly wasn't planning on filling his face any time soon, but for the quartet of Panadols that made up his lunch.

That he might be sick in another way, a way that neither rest nor medicine could cure, concerned him only distantly. Right now his biggest concern was making the hours fast forward until his wife came home, and made things okay again.

In the meantime he had to find something to do, read a book, write his next chapter, find a film –

Daniel frowned. His next chapter. What was that supposed to be on again? The frown deepened as he racked his brain and discovered he couldn't even remember what the previous one was about, and this something he'd only written two... three... how many days ago?

Feet heavy beneath him, the stairs creaked as Daniel made his ascent to the attic, passed remnants of – yesterday's? – broken glass, sat down in front of his laptop, and opened his manuscript.

He read the words in front of him, blinked, and read them again. If there'd been any colour left in him, it would have fled then. These words weren't his.

Back to the previous page. No luck.

Further. Retreat.

Wall after wall of terrifying text met his scrolling cursor, and none of it his.

Another page. Five. Ten. Beads of sweat broke out on Daniel's forehead as he glanced at the word count, and saw it about three times the size it ought to be. He kept scrolling, kept flicking his finger, searching, praying for a foothold, something of his own, something to cling to, and very well would have kept on like that interminably, if the batteries in his mouse didn't choose that exact moment to die.

She looks at me, and I at her, and in this moment we both know. I, her distaste for me, she, my fear of her. Rather than address this, she merely goes on.

"You say you don't love her, why do you think that is?"

I stare back at her, unfeeling. When was the last time I felt? She waits for a reply, patient, cunning. I know she'll use whatever I say against me. They always do. I can't be trusted to settle things for myself. Why else would I be here?

She notes my silence, disregards it. She looks into her journal, and without looking up, posits a question. "Do you think the child is yours?"

"What?" I ask, my chest suddenly constricting. How… how could she know that? Even I don't know that.

"Rosanna," she says simply. "Do you think she is your daughter?"

My mind is awhirl. Of course she is my daughter, how could she say such a thing? Just because I don't love her doesn't mean she isn't mine.

She does not wait for a reply, though I think I see the faint twist of a smile on her face. She knows she has gotten to me, and I know she won't let it end there.

"Has there been a paternity test?"

"Why would there be?" I demand, rising from my seat. "Who else would be the father but me?" I feel my pulse in my hands as well as my tongue, as her question still rings in my head. *Why would there be?*

"Oh Daniel," she says, then points off to my left with her pen, as the red ink leaks down onto her wrinkled hands, stains them.

I look to where she points, and freeze. There she is, standing beside me, her entire face as ink-stained as the old crone's wrists. Rosanna. She stares at me from under her curly blonde hair, as her eyes shine out like great orange beacons amidst so much red, and I wilt under her gaze.

"Look at her, Daniel."

"No."

"Look at her!"

Wincing, I submit, and look at the creature before me. Even her clothes aren't free from the ink, the green of her cloak soiled deep red. Through it all she stares back at me, unfazed. There is no animosity in that stare, just a simple question.

Do you really think I'm yours?

"Look at her, Daniel."

I look at her.

"Of course she's not yours. How could she be yours? Look at her."

I look at her, and for the first time, I see.

"She's beautiful."

I nod simply. Rosanna's stare doesn't change.

"She's perfect."

This particular passage ended there.

'What in the unholy fuck?' Daniel whispered.

What had he just read? What had he just *wrote*? Who was this woman, this "crone", and why did she make these claims?

And why do I believe them?

Fuck off. Fuck off. That voice wasn't his. It wasn't.

Whose is it then?

Daniel shut it out, shut all thoughts out, closed his eyes and tried to breathe. He didn't write this. He couldn't have. Never in a million years would he write something so... so...

So close to the truth?

'Get out of my head!'

Daniel's breathing was all over the place. What would Keira do, if she found out about this? What should *he* do, now that he had?

Bin it, bin the whole thing. *That* was his voice, now, and he rushed to comply. Fuck the novel, fuck everything, he needed his life back. Finger on trackpad, he closed the document, right-clicked on the icon and... hesitated.

There would be questions. If he up and erased the first thing he'd actually worked on in years, there'd have to be questions. There were 30,000 words here for God's sake – not including the recent finds – that was half a novel. Not to mention Keira had skimmed through some of it already to make sure the bits he'd based off Rosanna were above-board, what was he meant to say the next time she asked to see some more?

'*Oh yes, honey, unfortunately somewhere along the course of the novel I began to chart the course of my mental decline, and I'm afraid it didn't shine me in a particularly positive light, so I binned it.*' That didn't exactly cut it.

Daniel swallowed. If he couldn't delete it, he certainly couldn't leave it like this. Frantically, he skimmed the other pages before him, cringed at the cross-breed of diary-type entries and unsettling fantasies that emanated from the screen. Dream recollections, conversations overheard at the pub, shopping lists, anything that could be written about, he'd written down. But when? And *how*? Things had been going so well!

The more Daniel scanned, the more he started to notice little one-to-two sentence paragraphs crop up again and again throughout the unutterable ramblings, and they each delivered a similar, but slightly altered message, which chilled him to the core.

Go down to the woods.

If you go down.

Down to the woods today.

Down you go.

To the woods.

Be sure to go down to the woods today.

You have to go down to the woods.

Go down to the woods <u>TODAY</u>.

If you go down to the woods today be sure of a big surprise.

<u>TODAY'S</u> the day that <u>DADDY</u> bear has his picnic.

11

Rosanna. That had to be his primary thought. Picking Rosanna up from school, and not moss-laden vomit, spectral spirits, blighted newspaper articles and whatever-the-fuck had become of his novel. Rosanna, and keeping her nice and occupied until Keira came home.

She'd know what to do, she had to. Once he decided just exactly what it was he meant to tell her.

A flash of white caught his eye as his car sped round the bend towards the famine road, and Daniel screeched to a halt. A flash of white, and that primary thought was overridden.

It couldn't be. But as Daniel stared in disbelief at the sheaf of paper that floated weightlessly through the open gate to the old stone road, there wasn't a doubt in his mind. It belonged to the newspaper. How did not matter. Why did not matter. That the gate was open did not matter. Only that sheet of newspaper.

The car was turning before Daniel realised he'd given the command. Brittle stone crunched beneath the tyres as he wheeled his way through the gate, and followed as if in slow-motion the wayward page as it fluttered in the wind. Trees passed and shadows loomed but neither Daniel nor the paper noticed, eyes only for each other, like chasing a dance.

His parents died here.

It was the only thing that could have made him slow, the only thing to snap him out of the trance that twisting sheet had put him under. *Mother of one killed. Father missing.* His mother, at least, had died here. Just what had happened to his father, Daniel was no longer sure he wanted to know. On the road just ahead, the paper had settled amongst the stones.

Daniel tried to ignore the slickness of his palms as he slid his phone from his pocket. Who to call? He couldn't exactly ask Keira to pick Rosanna up in his stead, not while she was at actual work.

Joe, maybe, but he wasn't the kind to answer the phone, and he'd probably somehow collect the wrong child. Daniel rubbed his jaw as he scanned through his contacts and it became clear there was only one person who might be available, one person with a similar schedule to him. Not to mention she actually lived in the village. Daniel sighed. He never could make things easy on himself.

'Hello, Amy?'

'Yes…' the voice that answered was cautious, and Daniel had to swallow down the burn of jealousy it induced each time he heard it.

'Sorry to bother you, I was wondering if –'

'Excuse me, who is this?'

Daniel blinked. Did she really not have his phone number?

'It's Daniel,' he said, after a moment, and debated whether to throw his surname in alongside it.

'Oh. Hello Daniel. How are things?'

Terrible, obviously, if it had come to this. 'Good, good, yeah,' Daniel said. 'How are things with you? Is the filming going alright?'

There was a long pause on Amy's end. 'Well, shooting starts in January so...'

'Right, of course, sorry.' Daniel was grateful that at least she couldn't see the tomato his face had become. 'I'm at my wits end here.'

'You sound a bit scattered alright.'

That it was only a bit, Daniel took as a win. 'Listen, Amy, I hate to do this to you, but I've got some personal things I have to take care of and I was wondering if you could pick Rosanna up from school just now, provided it doesn't put you out too much? I just need someone to look after her while I try and sort this.'

'Now as in now, now?'

Daniel gulped, hoped she couldn't hear. On the road in front of him, the paper began to flutter. 'Yeah, now, now. Sorry.'

There came a sigh, and the sound of a chair being pushed back. 'Alright, I suppose. What you're doing sounds a bit more important than what I am, anyways. Anything she might need?'

'Thank you so much,' Daniel said, and would have closed his eyes in relief if not for the fear that doing so would see the newspaper wink out of existence ahead. 'She should have homework or something, don't worry, and if she gets fussy just give her some hot chocolate. Only one teaspoon of powder though or else she'll be in your hair for the next hour and –'

'Alright, homework, chocolate, got it. Anything else?'

'No, thank you. I shouldn't be too long anyways.'

'Sound,' Amy said, and then, almost as if it were an afterthought, 'Does Keira know what "personal business" you have to attend to, Daniel?'

Daniel grimaced, and his heart leapt as the page shot into the air once more. 'If she had anything to be worried about, do you really think I'd be calling you?'

Amy sat on this while Daniel started the car up again, re-commenced his pursuit.

'Fair enough, I guess.'

'Thanks so much, again.' Daniel barely heard himself, his ears twitched with each freshly crunched stone.

'Happy to do it,' Amy said. 'Maybe she can help with my writing.'

The line was cut and Daniel frowned briefly, unsure if this was a dig, then shook his head and refocused on the paper. Floating, gliding, twirling through the air, hypnotic, as the car followed on its stead, always a step or two behind, never quite catching up, always *just* out of –

What the bloody hell was he doing? Daniel killed the engine and unbuckled his seatbelt, stepped out into the cold winter air. Or, expected to, but the road was anything but. The trees provided shelter from more than just the rain, it seemed.

Daniel jumped as the car door clicked shut behind him, startled that so small a sound could be so greatly amplified here. Probably just nerves. The sheet lay forward, face down in the stones, and as Daniel stepped across to reach it, a faint gust of wind blew and took it into the air again.

Daniel put his hands on his hips. 'You've got to be fucking kidding me.'

Only a couple of metres ahead, Daniel strode on, but before he could get more than a few steps it was on its way once more. He watched its flight without moving, wondered how it could soar with such an abundant lack of wind, and at last it stopped, clung to the bark of a tree.

Winter air or not, Daniel grew cold when he saw what tree it was.

The sheet was A4 size, a printout as opposed to standard newspaper format, and it did a decent job of partially hiding the tree's scarred surface, but not enough. Maybe a real newspaper page would have been enough, but then, there were no real newspaper pages left, nor any microfilm. This was all he had, and crazy as it sounded, it knew it. Why else would it have chosen to wrap around this tree?

The only thing that shocked Daniel at this point was that he hadn't thought of it sooner. Of course it was this one. This the only one with any significant damage to its surface, all the others' damage lay firmly underneath. Fingers encircled round the corners of the sheet, stripped it from the bark, but Daniel no longer cared what it said.

This was where they died. Where *she* died, and him too. Whether or not he'd ever find out for sure, this tree had taken them from him. He'd walked past it how many times, with either Keira or Rosanna, right alongside? Unseeing, or not wanting to see. That scarring, hip-length from the forest floor, Keira had even brought it to his attention, years past.

'*It looks more like a dent than someone going at it with an axe.*'

A dent.

Daniel ran his fingertips along the dead wood, dry and jagged.

A wound.

Emotion came all at once, not a wave but a tsunami, and the weight of it knocked him back as he sank to the stony ground. Here was why he'd grown up without a mum or dad. Here was why he'd spent the best years of his life in a house he hated, with a woman he feared, who lied to him, who wouldn't even tell half-truths, who let him suffer alone in silence. A woman who'd fucked up any ounce of nurturing he'd had so badly that he was doing the same to his own daughter. Here. This tree. This dent. This wound. It felt more like his reflection than anything he'd seen in the mirror. On the rough stones that littered the forest floor, Daniel's vision blurred, and he cried a sob as silent as the trees themselves.

After some time, a minute, ten, an hour, Daniel didn't know, he pulled himself to his feet. The newspaper sheet hung limply in his hand, and he was tempted to drop it. He didn't want to know anymore, he didn't care anymore, he'd had enough hurting for one day, all he wanted was to go home, and hug his wife.

But the paper being what it was, and Daniel being who he was, he couldn't simply let it go. As he flipped the page it occurred to him for the first time that he might be met with the incomprehensible scrawlings of some random article, but before the thought was fully formed, he found himself staring at the front page of one of the June editions of the *Herald* itself. Daniel read the leading headline.

He read it again.

A third time, and then he let the page fall from his grasp, unable, incapable of reading any more. His hurting was not done yet. His hurting had only begun.

There came another breeze, slightly stronger than the last, and Daniel turned numbly toward it. With the current came that sensation of eyes on him, something he was used to on this road by now, which was why when he lifted his gaze and found it locked in the stare of another, he nearly fell to the ground all over again.

About fifteen metres down the road stood a man, motionless as he watched Daniel. Even as every natural instinct screamed at him to run, to hide, to flee, recognition flashed in his eyes. By the man's grey hair, he was some years older than Daniel, and the beard confirmed it, rough and ragged. It was the same man from town.

Without realising, Daniel had taken three steps forward. Only then did he notice the flecks of green scattered throughout that dry and dusty hair, the bits of shrub and moss that permeated his beard. He hadn't looked like this before.

Another step, and Daniel saw the foliage extended far beyond the man's hair. In sporadic patches it lined his cloak and boots, wove in and out of his trouser legs, ensnaring him. The full detail of his dishevelment revealed to Daniel, he stopped short, the distance between them halved.

Neither spoke, only stared. For once, the lump choking Daniel's throat was entirely natural.

'Dad?'

As soon as the word was out the man's eyes widened, though there was no way he could have heard, not from this distance, Daniel's voice was only a whisper. From beneath their bearded embrace, chapped lips fell open, and a single tear fell down his weathered face.

Daniel never would have guessed it would be something so small that sent him running in terror in the end.

His life was a lie, he knew that now, as he restarted the engine, only looking backwards, refusing to glimpse anything this side of his shoulder. Not just his life, the whole world was a lie, and Granny Cawley was the only one telling truths after all. The world wasn't his dream, it was hers. Her nightmare.

Dimly aware that the sky was darkening around him as he turned the car into gear and sped back down the road, the light draining from the forest at a rate that shouldn't be possible, Daniel's thoughts had time only for the other impossible thing he'd just seen.

Crying. A single tear, streaking down a face all too similar to his own. Yellow.

Sap.

10

It was night time. It shouldn't be, but it was. The digital clock to the left of the steering wheel hinted at the possibility, and the black abyss that threatened to crush Daniel overhead confirmed it. Night, when not half an hour ago he'd set out to collect Rosanna.

So many thoughts crashed madly about his head that he may as well have had none at all. His father was alive, but he was one of… one of *them*. How could that be? How could that *actually* be? It couldn't. It simply couldn't. Just like Stephen last night, it wasn't real, it didn't happen, he hadn't seen it.

Except he had. Try as he might to rid himself of it, the mental image of that single, sticky yellow tear was forever scarred into his memory. His father, the… the *tree*-person.

TODAY'S the day that DADDY bear has his picnic.

Daniel shuddered. Who was doing this to him? And why? What had he ever done to deserve it? And how the fuck was it night time?

There was only one option, besides himself, but he couldn't bring himself to believe it any more than he could that. It couldn't be him, he felt the same as he always had. Crazy people knew they were crazy, or at least they had some idea of it, right? But, he did have some idea of it. Daniel rubbished the thought. He couldn't start doubting himself, not now, but then, he couldn't believe in *them* either. They weren't real. They were myth, folklore, fantasy, they didn't exist in a grove not twenty minutes' walk from his home. They weren't real.

Were they?

The mug. The stairs. The vomit. Stephen. The wink. None of those seemed real either, none of those should be allowed to be real,

117

but they'd all happened, he'd seen them all. Just like he'd seen his father, and his tears of sap.

Daniel's hands shook as he turned the car into the driveway. It was half-past eleven, and all the lights in the house were on. How the hell was he meant to explain this to Keira?

Before he'd even had time to get out of the car, let alone formulate an excuse, the front door was open and she was rushing outside. She threw her arms around him, and hugged him close with a ferocity he hadn't felt in a long, long time. As the lovely apple-scent of her shampoo filled his lungs, Daniel closed his eyes and crumpled into her.

'Where were you?' Keira asked into his chest. 'I called you a hundred times and you wouldn't answer, Amy said... said...'

'It's okay,' Daniel whispered, but the black sky above named him a liar. 'I'm sorry.'

'Where were you?' There was fear in her voice as she repeated the question, but anger too.

As cold wind battered Daniel, protected by the forest no longer, he shivered. 'Come inside and we'll talk.'

The warmth and familiarity of the house settled him a touch, but only a touch. He stared into the ashes of the empty hearth, and wondered, if it was Granny Cawley here with him, and not Keira, would he be more likely to tell the truth?

'I'm waiting, Daniel.' The hardness in her voice was belied by her red and swollen eyes, her quaking lip, the need to be reassured.

'Okay,' Daniel said softly, and sat at the table. She followed suit, and her watery eyes met his wild pupils. Was he about to do this? Could he lie, right to her face? He'd have liked to take solace in the fact that doing so would protect her, but it wouldn't, not really. It would be protecting himself. 'I don't really know how to say this –'

And he didn't, because a buzz from his pocket disrupted his flow of speech.

'Oh, so you had your phone with you the whole time then?' Keira asked, anger flashing again.

Daniel barely heard her, the vibrations were so intense, sending pins and needles down his leg. He reached for it and the tremors passed into his hand, coursed through to his arm and shoulder, visibly rattling them.

'What the hell is wrong with it?' Keira's voice was quiet astonishment now.

On the screen, a mish-mash of colours danced out at Daniel, spazzing with a fervency he'd never witnessed before. Beneath the phone's glitchy surface, the UI was bombarded by notifications: system update, system error, system-fucking-breakdown.

Daniel continued to stare in dumb silence, to the point that Keira reached across the table and took it from him. As the tremors passed to her, her eye's widened.

'What did you do to it?'

'I have no idea,' Daniel muttered. 'Give it here.'

Keira handed it back, eager to be rid of it, and Daniel tried to shut it down by holding the power button, to no avail.

'Try taking the battery out.'

Daniel's phone was an older Samsung model which meant the battery wasn't built-in like newer editions and he could still do so. He popped the back off, exposing the battery, and went to pluck it out with his thumb.

'Shit!' he hissed, recoiling as he dropped the phone to the floor and sucked his thumb.

'What? What is it?' Keira asked, standing up.

'The thing's hotter than a stove!' Daniel took his thumb from his mouth and saw a thin white line had formed just above his fingernail, like he'd burnt it on a baking tray. On the floor, the phone had stopped buzzing, the battery knocked out of place from its impact with the tiles, but now they were faced with a new problem.

'Jesus, Daniel, look!'

Daniel was looking. Smoke wafted out from the battery as what should be dark grey glowed an ominous red. If that were a lithium battery…

'Keira, get back!' Daniel barked. She was standing right in the battery's path should it go off, and based on the ever deepening red glow that *should* was looking very much like a *when*.

Keira did as he said, shuffled round to Daniel's side of the table as he ushered the two of them towards the kitchen door, the smoke thickening as the air grew choked.

'Daniel, what the hell is –'

CRACK.

The battery erupted into a ball of flame, rising to a metre off the ground. Shrapnel flew in all directions and Daniel turned to shield Keira as something crashed behind them.

'Are you okay?' he asked, after a few frantic seconds. He'd managed to survive the blast unscathed by the feel of it, he only hoped Keira had got through the same.

'Yeah, I'm fine,' Keira said, dusting herself down. 'Jesus Daniel, why the hell did it do that?'

'Must have been a lithium battery,' Daniel said, as if that was anywhere near an appropriate explanation. 'It probably overheated.'

'Daniel...' Keira said quietly, and her fingers gripped his arm. 'Look.'

Daniel followed where she was pointing, and his breath caught short. 'Oh.'

The crash he'd heard. It was Spot's fishbowl. The little red goldfish lay in a puddle on the floor amongst shards of broken glass.

Keira covered her mouth with a hand. 'Is he...'

Daniel went over to the broken bowl and got on his knees before it, careful not to put his weight down on any shattered glass. Spot didn't move, nor did he flop, or writhe, or gasp for water. Spot was dead.

Daniel picked him up and looked at his tiny corpse. At some point, he had become a *he*. He hadn't always been. He was neither male or female, back when Keira had won him. He'd transcended gender. That was the day he'd proposed to her, and Spot had been like Keira's ring to him.

The tears that stung Daniel's eyes surprised him. The little guy had never grown to the size of his arm after all, and never would.

'Daniel…' Keira said again, but that was all she could say. She stood behind him, placed a comforting hand on his shoulder.

Daniel was about to rise, about to bring Spot into the bathroom to his final resting place, when a glint of light caught his eye, and he paused. A shard of glass had lodged itself right between his gills, straight through the centre of his namesake, that little white spot, so pure amongst the red. Not quite sure why he did it, Daniel gripped the glass and gave it a tug. It slid out with ease, but strangely, no blood came with it. Something must have been clogging the flow, part of the shard of glass that had broken off, or a piece of the shrapnel itself. Daniel held the fish up to his eyeline so that he could better look into the wound.

'Daniel, please, just put him down, I can't…' Keira's voice was choked with emotion, but Daniel was unable to stop himself. He needed to find the source of that blockage, he needed to know why his goldfish was dead.

Bending back Spot's cold and scaly skin, Daniel stuck his fingernail deeper into the wound. Keira gave a soft moan from behind him, and the grip on his arm tightened. He rooted around for a couple of seconds before he felt something brush the burn mark on his thumb. *There*.

The fatal weapon was very small, very thin, but Daniel hadn't cut his nails in a long time, and he pried it loose with a gentle pull. As the culprit came forth, so too did the blood, and Daniel's thumb and forefinger came back stained with red. What he'd pried loose was not a shard of glass, nor a piece of shrapnel, however. Keira, who'd turned away, pressed her head into his shoulder, did not see what he'd retrieved. Daniel stared at it dumbly.

It was a blade of grass.

*

There they were again, those water-stains. Some bedroom ceilings had posters, some had glow-in-the-dark stars, while his had these. Sometimes, times like this, they looked like faces, like people grinning down at him, laughing. He wished he was able to see what it was they found so funny.

After he'd gotten over the shock of seeing that thin blade of grass slip out of Spot's lifeless corpse and all the blood that came with it, Daniel had hidden the item from Keira. Like many of his actions lately, he couldn't say why he did it, he didn't have a reason, it was all instinctual now, and those instincts told him that he couldn't let her see it.

When they'd finally got to talking, after Spot's brief funeral and the cleaning up of broken glass, Daniel's mind was so exhausted that he didn't even have to think of the lies, they just came to him.

He'd gone to the library to read up on the crash like she'd suggested, and ended up spending hours cycling through old papers until he found what he was looking for. He'd turned his phone off then, and left it that way. Once he'd learned the truth of his parents' accident, that it had been right here, in the forest by their home, he left the library and went there by himself, lost track of time. After that, things were a haze. He'd gone to the village and went to the beach after all, though he didn't come across Stephen or Mary, just sat in the sand and stared at the waves, thinking. He knew he should have called but he couldn't, there wasn't anything he was able to say, he just had to be alone.

'Okay,' Keira had said after it all.

'Is it?'

'Well, no, not really. You can't leave us here like that, without knowing where you are. You don't know how worried I –' her voice caught, and she let out a couple of haggard breaths before speaking again. 'You just can't do that. You have to tell me things, okay? You have to tell me where you are.'

Daniel nodded, thinking of his father, thinking of the newspaper headline. 'Okay, I will.'

The lies came very easy indeed.

The sound of the toilet flushing pulled him back to the present, and he turned his gaze away from the smiling faces towards Keira's decidedly tremulous one. Immediately, Daniel sensed something was wrong, perhaps more wrong than anything that had gone before it today. Keira slumped against the doorframe, and brought her left hand to her forehead. In her right, she held something.

Daniel saw what it was.

Keira saw that he saw, and she lowered her head, bit her lip.

'Well?' Daniel croaked.

Keira looked up at him with the world's saddest smile and raised the stick so that he could see. The faint light of the moon shone through their bedroom window and lit on a plastic pink pregnancy test.

The little plus at its centre said more than either of them ever could.

9

It was a wet morning, and windy too, but in the graveyard behind Ballyfarreg's parish church, Daniel hardly noticed. The grey sky overhead paired suitably with the polished marble of his grandmother's headstone.

IN LOVING MEMORY OF MARIE CAWLEY
GRANDMOTHER
MOTHER
FRIEND
JUNE 5, 1929
DECEMBER 17, 2007

December 17th. Her anniversary. He'd missed it, last year, buried beneath the chaos of the Christmas period. For the next few weeks it hadn't sat right with him, forgetting like that, and he'd always meant to come and drop off some flowers or even just drop his head by to say hello, but after a while, he'd forgotten that too. Maybe she hadn't.

'Are you haunting me?' Daniel asked. 'Is that what this is?'

For her part, old Granny Cawley didn't seem to have heard, but then she could be positively clawing at the coffin and the noise would never have reached him.

Daniel sighed. 'I don't know what's going on anymore. You used to always seem like you were the only one who did.'

But for the faint lapping of the wind, all was silent.

'I'm... scared. I don't know if the things that are happening to me are actually happening.' Daniel thought of the banging on the door, thought of the moss. 'They seem it at the time, but then whenever I look back, I think, that can't have actually happened, can it?'

He thought of his father, of losing an entire day in the space of a few minutes.

'What if I'm dreaming it all? What if I have insomnia, or psychosis? What if the times I think I'm awake, I'm actually not, and the other way around?'

The attic. The shattered pint glass.

'I can't tell her the truth. I don't want her to be scared of me. But I can't keep... *I'm* scared of me, right now. But not just of me, I'm scared of it all. If I'm not crazy, if this is happening, then why me? What else didn't you tell me?'

Daniel stared at the little plot of grass, swaying in the breeze.

'You were my mum, you know that right?'

A faint knock? A whisper on the wind? No, only silence.

'For so long, you were all I had. You were all I knew. The things you taught me… that's not the way things should be. You can't… you can't lie to those who love you, and still expect them to love you, it's not fair. Because they will. They will still love you, they can't help themselves. So you shouldn't keep things from them. You shouldn't.'

Daniel's eyes welled, and he turned his gaze upon the clouds.

'But I can't tell her this, because I don't know what *this* is. You never told me. You always knew, and you never told me. You were my mum, but I was never your son.'

His right hand slipped into his jacket pocket, caressed the object stowed inside.

'I'm more like you than I'd like. Rosanna, she… I can't be to her what you were to me. I can't go it on my own, like you did. I don't know what you found out, what you knew or what you didn't, but I think I know enough myself now. I know I have to tell someone, because if I don't, I will go crazy, if I'm not already. It just can't be Keira, not yet. Not until I know she won't get hurt.'

Daniel knelt, and with his free hand ran his fingers through the rain-spotted grass. With the other, he pulled what he'd brought with him out from his pocket, and laid it gently amongst the others, just the same, but for the red mar at its tip.

'He was pretty good, as far as pets go. I always wondered why you never let us have any of our own.'

With that, he rose, and with the faint taste of iron in his throat, went to have a talk.

*

'What do you want?' Amy's arms were folded as she stood in the doorway of her two-storey home, one of the finer amongst a litany of more-than-fine residences that lined Ballyfarreg's sapphire coast.

'Can I come in?' Daniel asked.

'Why? Here to pick up your daughter? Oh that's right, you're –' she made a show of checking her watch '– about three days too late.'

Daniel felt the burn of red flush to his head and grimaced. 'I know. I'm sorry. But I really do need to talk to you. It's important.'

'Well, considering I no longer believe a word that comes out of your mouth, we can probably do that right here. Nice and quick.'

Daniel's head dipped low as he fiddled with his fingers. 'Please, Amy. You're the only one I can tell.'

She watched him a moment, considering, and Daniel felt very much under the microscope. Was that how Rosanna felt, when he'd followed her around with the notepad?

'Alright,' Amy said, and backed away from the door. 'Come in and shut that behind you. But I swear to God if you're about to tell me you cheated on Keira then you won't live to see it open again.'

Daniel nodded as he followed her instructions and then herself into the living room. 'That seems fair. I haven't, by the way.'

'I'm glad,' Amy said, and reached into a large oak cabinet, from which she pulled a litre-bottle of Redbreast. 'Drink?'

Daniel's eyes flicked to the clock. 'It's half-one...' and combine that with what happened in Kelleher's with Joe, he definitely shouldn't. 'So yeah, go on.'

Amy's smile was more polite than amused as she handed over the glass and motioned for Daniel to sit. Once he had, he took a swig, and grimaced.

'So...?' Amy asked, sitting across from him. It was only then Daniel noticed she wore no more than a slip of a tank top and some very short-shorts. Careful not to flush red again, he averted his eyes towards the contents of his glass and took a second sip, much better this time.

'Well, I –'

'Wait,' Amy said, and her voice was so severe it gave Daniel pause. 'You better not be out here picking up Rosanna, are you?' Her gaze was locked on the drink she'd just poured him.

'What? No, she's going to Sam's after. You hardly think I'm that bad, do you?'

Amy merely shrugged.

'Alright, also fair,' Daniel said, and took another swig for good measure. 'I'm here because I need your advice. Something's going on and I don't know what to do about it, and I need your help.'

Amy took the first sip of her own, frowning. 'Why do you want my help? I thought you hated me.'

129

Daniel caught himself on the very brink of saying, *I do*, and covered it with a slight cough. 'What gave you that idea?'

A raised eyebrow was enough to set him back on course.

'Alright. Why you? Because you're the only one crazy enough to believe it, and even if you don't, at least you'll act out of Keira's best interests, and not my own.'

Amy pursed her lips. 'Strange.'

'What is?'

'That you'd consider insanity to be an aide and not a hindrance,' she said, and sipped. 'But do, please, go on.'

Daniel rubbed his forehead. 'Do you always have to be so…'

'Relentless? Not particularly, but I find it's more fun that way. You were saying?'

'Right.' He was saying. 'It started, I think, with a mug.'

Amy blinked. 'A mug?'

'A mug.'

'Well fuck,' Amy muttered. 'Sounds like we're gonna need another glass.'

It took three glasses in the end, each, before Daniel finally got it all out of him. The stairs descending, and the mug. The forest, the famine road, and his granny's stories. The attic at night, and breath on his neck. The homeless man, the familiarity, how sure he'd been that it was his father. Feeling hazy, time slipping him by, standing by the car one moment, transported halfway home the next. Pints with Joe, and throwing up a glob of moss. The newspaper archives, *Mother of one dead, Father missing*. Losing them in the wind. Stephen, and not-Stephen. His reflection winking. Returning to the library, and everything destroyed. What had become of his novel, the passages about Rosanna – though somewhat censored, just to be safe – *If you go down to the woods today be sure of a big surprise.* Going down. Finding the newspaper, finding the truth, or, some of it, and the tree that his parents crashed into. The ghost of his father, and his tears of sap. Time falling through, day then suddenly night, his phone erupting in his pocket, Spot.

'… and then she came in with the test and just sort of held it up to me. I think I thought I was going to die, then. I'd rather have died, than seen the look on her face.'

Amy, who'd barely spoken a word since he began, leant back in her chair, and drank what was left of her third glass. 'Fuck.'

Daniel winced. 'What do you think I should do?'

'What do I think you should do?' Amy puffed out her cheeks, ran a hand down her face. 'Jesus. Right, just, before I go any further, you're not *on* anything, are you? You didn't look for divine inspiration in a bad batch of shrooms or something?'

'Not that I'm aware of.'

'Okay,' Amy said. 'Probably would have made things a hell of a lot easier if you were. Right, everything you just told me, all the… spooky shit, we're just gonna put that to one side for now, alright?'

'Alright…'

Amy poured a fourth glass for herself, and the same for Daniel. As she handed it back across, she asked, 'Your book, this new one, what's it about?'

Daniel blinked. 'It's about… it's about the famine road. And faeries. Why?'

'No,' Amy said, 'it's about your family.'

For so long, he'd been the one doing all the talking. Now that it was Amy's turn, he realised he had no idea how to respond.

'The main character, Eileen, she's Rosanna right? Don't shake your head, Keira told me. She's worried about that and she's worried about you,' Amy looked him up and down, 'As well she should be. But, again, leaving that aside for now, you said that every time you write things get foggy, or that you don't remember writing at all. These "time slips" you mentioned, and they're followed by you seeing things that may not actually be there.'

'That's not –'

'Let me finish. You're writing about your family. About your great-great-grandfather, and, let's face it, about your daughter. The things you've been seeing, they're all your family too. Stephen, your father, the newspaper article. Your worlds are colliding. You're writing about freaky things happening to your relatives, and so now you think your relatives are causing freaky things. That's the way I see it anyways.'

Daniel frowned. To a certain extent, some of what Amy said made sense, but it didn't cover everything. 'What about the moss in my vomit? Or the wink? Or–'

'Daniel, listen to me. You're tired. You've overworked yourself, and you need sleep. Take it from someone who knows what they're talking about. Christ, have you read my last book? *Autumn Eve*? Now that's something that could have done with a bad batch of shrooms, and not the three lines of white needed to get through each chapter. When I finally got it done, I found I didn't need them so much anymore. Guess it was the writing I was addicted to.'

Daniel mulled this over for a moment. 'I'm not exactly sure that it's the same.'

'Well of course it's not the same, but what did you expect? I can only give answers to what I know, and what you're going on about, I don't really know much about that do I? I do know you need a break. A break from work, a break from stress. Stop writing. Spend time with your family. You don't have any deadlines, so what's stopping you? If you carry on like this, you'll kill yourself or worse. Take a break, and if it's still going on, see a therapist or something.' She shook what was left of the whiskey bottle. 'My homeopathic remedies will only get you so far.'

Daniel found he was nodding, found he might actually be agreeing. 'You're right,' he muttered.

'What's that?' Amy asked, and a wry smile broke out.

'I said you're right,' Daniel said again. It wasn't even difficult.

Amy grinned. 'Never thought I'd hear those words from you.'

'Never thought I'd be saying them.'

The two looked at each other for a moment, saying nothing, and in that nothing, Daniel passed his immense gratitude onto her with words he could never speak. A slight tilt of Amy's head told him she understood.

'You know, in another life we might have been friends,' she said.

Daniel smiled softly. 'Thank you, Amy. Really.'

She looked him up and down once more, and then at the half-finished glass on the table. 'Now, do you want to try explain to Keira why you're absolutely steamboats in my house at three o'clock in the afternoon, or should I?'

*

As soon as the front door to Amy's house shut behind them, Keira's smile slipped.

'What's up?' Daniel asked as he fumbled with his seat belt, trying very hard not to slur either word.

'What's up?' Keira repeated, staring straight out at the road ahead. 'Nothing Daniel, nothing at all. This is just perfectly normal, isn't it?'

'How do you mean?' Daniel asked, and even as he did, his head whirled.

'You just show up to Amy's house, a place you've never even been to, to "apologise" and then the two of you get shitfaced together and you tell her I'm pregnant. I mean what the fuck,

Daniel? Even if we forget everything else, why the hell would you tell her that?'

Daniel's features crinkled as he looked out at the waves. Why he'd actually told her, he couldn't say for sure. Why he'd told Keira he'd told her, well, he needed an excuse for the whole shit-facing, didn't he? Only he may have horribly misjudged how she'd respond.

'I haven't even known a week and you think you can – ugh.' Keira's hands tensed on the wheel, but she didn't go on.

'I'm sorry,' Daniel muttered. 'I… it just slipped out. I should have waited. I'm sorry.'

Keira bit her lip to stop it shaking, eyes still only for the road. 'Yeah, you should have. Especially when we don't know… when we haven't discussed all the options.'

Just as Daniel had begun to get his head under control, it reeled all over again. 'What do you mean, "all the options"?' he asked slowly.

Keira's jaw set, and her voice hardened. 'You know what I mean.'

Daniel fell back into his seat, stomach suddenly aswarm with butterflies. 'You don't mean you're thinking about…?'

'Of course I'm thinking about it,' Keira said, and turned to glance at Daniel. When she saw the way he looked back at her, her face crumpled. 'Don't look at me like that. Don't fucking look at me like that.'

Daniel blinked, stunned by her tears. 'Like what?'

'Like I'm a monster,' Keira said, and then she started to cry.

Daniel could only watch from his own private bubble of turbulent emotions as her whole frame shook in the seat. 'Don't cry…'

'I can't believe you told her.' Keira shook her head. 'I just can't.'

'I didn't know –'

'I can't, now,' Keira cut across him. From her ever-thickening pools, she looked him in the eye. 'You know that, right? People would know. They'd talk. They'd look at me just like you are.'

Daniel struggled for words, blinked away tears of his own. 'I didn't – it's only Amy, Keira, who's she going to tell?'

'Anyone! She could tell fucking anyone, Daniel, and pretty soon the whole world will know, and I don't… I can't…'

'What?' Daniel asked softly.

Keira let out a long, shuddering breath. 'I can't watch you go through that again. It almost broke me.'

For a moment there was only silence, and the thunderous beat of Daniel's heart. She'd never told him anything like this before. 'What do you mean?'

Keira rolled her eyes. 'Oh come on, like you don't know.'

Daniel stared back, unspeaking, until she shook her head.

'Rosanna, Daniel. Rosanna.'

If he weren't already seated, Daniel was certain he would have collapsed then. His legs had gone completely numb, and his voice was a breathless whisper. 'What about her?'

Keira's entire being was a trembling mess as she tried to keep her eyes on the road. 'Daniel... I love you more than anything, *anything*, but what you went through with her, what *I* went through, I... I can't do it again. I can't watch you go in on yourself like you did, become a shell of a person. You almost stopped speaking. I was so scared and I didn't have anyone to go to. I didn't have you. I... I thought I'd lost you.' She looked over at him, her voice thick as the tears ran down her cheeks. 'I can't lose you. I can't.'

Daniel reached over and squeezed her hand, was shocked by how forcefully she gripped onto it in return. He stared at her in awe. She would do anything for him. She was the most incredible mother he'd ever seen, and yet she was willing to do that, for him. Never in a million years would he ever deserve her.

'It won't be like that this time,' Daniel said. 'I promise you it won't.'

Keira's lips continued to work, but no sound came out.

'You're not going to do that for me, Keira. You're not. You'll either end up hating me forever or hanging onto my every word. I'm not worth it, trust me.'

Keira's chest hitched, and her voice spoke quiet damnation. 'You are to me.'

Daniel looked at her a moment longer, then at the road in front, endless asphalt surrounded by empty fields. 'Pull over.'

'What? Why?'

'Just do.'

She did, and before the car was even fully stopped, Daniel was out of his passenger side and sweeping round to Keira's door. He pulled it open.

'Come here.'

'What?'

'Come here.'

The moment she unbuckled her seatbelt, Daniel reached in, tugged her out of the vehicle and into his arms. After a few brief seconds of quiet embrace, the crying started again, both of them this time, and they buried their heads in each other's shoulders.

'I love you so much.'

'I love you too.'

'I don't ever want to lose you.'

'You won't, I promise.'

'I can't do this, if that's what will happen.'

'It won't. I swear it won't.'

Keira's breath was ragged against his chest. 'I want to believe you. I *so* want to believe you, but sometimes I see the way you look at her and it's like… like…' she fell into him once more.

'Like what?' Daniel whispered.

'It's like you're scared of her.'

Daniel's stomach churned. Careful not to let it show, he tried to disguise his unease with a gentle laugh. 'Is that all? Of course I'm scared of her, Keira, I'm terrified. She's a little person. Our little person. What if she ever got hurt or –'

'No.'

Daniel's faux-mirth dried up. 'No?'

'No. You're not scared in that way, that she might hurt herself.' Keira pulled back from him, and looked him dead in the eyes. 'You look scared that she might hurt you.'

8

Daniel stared into the mirror, and saw only himself. Good. Sort of. Rolling up the length of his sleeve, he twirled his arm around to examine both sides, first his right, then his left. Nothing that his eye could see, and nothing that the mirror should choose to reveal. That should be good, too, but for the fact that of late, seeing very much did not equate to believing.

His arms *felt* wrong. There was no other way to put it. They were stiff at all times, and at night, when he couldn't sleep, when he was faced with those laughing, watery faces yet again, they itched something horrendous.

If it were just his arms, he might have forgiven it, chalked it off to exhaustion, burnout like Amy said, but it wasn't. All morning, he'd been phlegmy, that was what had brought him into the bathroom in the first place, and he stared at the result of that phlegm in the otherwise clear white sink. Bright yellow, and thick. Syrupy. Almost like…

'Daniel?'

Keira. Thank Christ for Keira, the only thing in his life that actually made sense.

In the kitchen, she looked down at her phone.

'You called?'

Keira glanced up at him. 'You know the way Amy was going to drop Rosanna out from Sam's as well as drive your car home because she's actually not a terrible person?'

'I feel like a comment here will incriminate me somehow…'

'Yeah, well, doesn't matter anyway.' She tossed him her phone. 'Your car won't start.'

Daniel frowned down at the contents of Amy's message. *Tried everything. Even looked under hood, nothing wrong that I can see. Help plz.*

'Do you think that it's because…' Daniel began, and Keira turned to him inquisitively. '…she's a woman?'

'I will kill you.'

'I know you won't.'

Keira narrowed her eyes at him and he narrowed them back in turn, a pair of gunslingers at high noon, until Daniel kissed her on the nose.

'Joking, obviously.'

'I know.'

'It's because she's gay.'

They picked Rosanna up from her sleepover on the way out to Amy's as opposed to the way home. It was the first she'd ever been on, Keira had decided that she needed something to pick her spirits up after Spot's untimely demise, and, contrary to what either of them expected, Caitríona, Sam's mum, was in no way eager to part with her.

'She's just got the most incredible calming influence on him. I don't think I've ever had a sleepover as quiet.'

Rosanna shied away from the praise as she hurried into the back of the car, but as soon as Caitríona's attention was away from her and back on Keira, she was all smiles and grins, waving a colouring pencil out the window at Sam as he hid behind his mother's leg.

'What's that you've got there?' Daniel asked as the women chatted.

'Sam got me turr-kwoize, I didn't have any before.'

'Oh,' Daniel said, eyeing the blonde boy sidelong. 'You know I'd have gotten you some turquoise, if you asked.'

Rosanna shook her head. 'It's not the same.'

Barely five and already the boys were winning her over with shiny things. Daniel grinned down at the lad, winked. 'Get her green next time kid, that's her favourite.'

Sam flushed a bright red and sought refuge further behind Caitríona, who said her goodbyes to the three of them and off they went again.

At Amy's house for the second time in two days, the woman was outside before Keira had fully parked the car. 'I just don't know what's wrong with it. Sorry to cause you all this hassle.'

Keira rubbished her. 'Nonsense, you were willing to drive all the way out to us, no reason we can't do the same. Come on,' she said, and took Rosanna's hand, 'why don't the three of us go inside for some hot chocolate while Daniel has a look to see if he can spot anything different?'

'What, no hot chocolate for me?' Daniel asked.

'You know the rules. Women and homosexuals first,' Keira said, and left him standing there, tongue-in-cheek, as a very excited Rosanna showed off her new pen to an equally bemused Amy.

Once they were inside, Daniel turned to face his latest problem. Car troubles, at least, were the kind that did not discriminate. Your life could be as figured-out as it was ever going to be, or completely falling apart at the seams, and that engine with four wheels would still find a way to suck money out of you.

He slid into the driver's seat and put the key in the ignition, turned it. Nothing. No coughs, no splutters, not even the wheeze of a dying vehicle. Simply nothing. Rinse and repeat a couple of times to the same result, Daniel sighed and hopped out, made his way over to the bonnet to see if there was anything Amy had missed. He was the furthest thing from a technician, but surely if something were obviously wrong he'd be able to –

Daniel stepped back from the open hood, and stared. Maybe, *maybe*, he'd expected a few things awry, spilt engine fluid, frayed cables, a dented battery, whatever. Not this. There was no way he ever could have expected this.

That fact he'd made it to Amy's in this car without killing himself was nothing short of a miracle. Everywhere his eye landed, foliage screamed bright-green back up at him. Grass, burnt brown at the tips, lined the entire interior, from radiator to engine. Brambles wrapped their way around the engine itself, meshed with choking vines and ivy that enveloped objects he should know the name of but didn't. The engine-coolant water had turned to a deep, bloody orange, and the battery had been pierced through and woven multiple times by the same bramble that warped the engine, as well as yellow gorse and thistle. Everywhere he looked, green, or orange, or brown, or yellow, never grey, everywhere wild, everyway crazy.

Amy's text. *Even looked under hood, nothing wrong that I can see.*

Daniel scrambled back from the car, and slammed the bonnet shut. She'd seen none of it. This didn't have anything to do with his writing, no amount of rest could save him from… from…

'How's it looking?'

Daniel's head whipped round to see Keira standing in the doorway, and his heart plummeted. He could feel the sweat on his forehead, could only pray that she couldn't see it.

143

'Fine,' he heard himself say from far away. 'Nothing wrong that I can see.' Maybe he should ask her to look under it herself, maybe if he was with her when she did it, then she'd see it too and – No! He was keeping her away from this, he had to.

Keira, one eye inside the house, didn't notice anything amiss. 'Still won't start though?'

'Won't seem to.' Was that normal? Was his voice normal? How did he sound, usually?

'Have you tried jump-starting it?'

'Yup,' Daniel lied. Was he fuck putting electric currents anywhere near that mess of green. 'No dice.'

Keira looked at him, then looked at her own car as if to say, *you got that done pretty quick*, and shrugged. 'Guess you'll have to call someone. Hot chocolate?'

Daniel nodded. 'Please.'

*

As Daniel put Keira's phone down, still yet to replace his own, arrangements for the car to be towed made, she and Amy discussed New Year's plans.

'I just think we should do something, you know?' Amy said. 'Even if it's something small. Not town though, I'm sick of all the young ones off their heads.'

'We could do something, couldn't we Daniel?' Keira asked.

Daniel didn't hear right away, his eyes fixed on the layer of melted marshmallows that sat atop his hot chocolate, scanning for foreign objects.

'Daniel?'

'Huh? Sorry, I mean, yeah, I suppose.'

Keira gave him a searching look then shook her head and turned back to Amy. 'See what happens when you let him drink?'

'Typical man,' Amy said. 'What were you thinking, like a small house party or something?'

'Something like that, yeah. Only don't say house party, it makes us sound fifteen.'

'A dinner *soirée*,' Daniel heard himself mumble.

Keira looked at him oddly again, and Daniel turned his gaze onto Rosanna, who was busy putting her new turquoise pencil to use. He wished he could find something so mind-numbingly cathartic.

'It could be fun,' Amy said. 'Though you may be prevented from taking part in the festivities.'

'Why would I – Oh, right.' Keira looked down at her belly. 'Shit.'

Daniel glanced over at it too, and back to Rosanna, yesterday's conversation still fresh in his mind. On the page, she scrawled a rough oblong shape, which seemed to be the primary focus of the turquoise.

'That doesn't mean you can't have fun though, right?' Amy said, and pursed her lips. 'Where do doctors stand on edibles?'

Keira snorted. 'Best not risk it, I imagine.'

'Shame that.'

Daniel watched the slow motion of Rosanna's hands, the way she constantly fidgeted with the page with her left hand even as she scribbled on with her right. He wasn't scared of her, that he should have to come out and deny it, even to himself, was ridiculous. She was just a little kid. *His* little kid.

'What are you drawing there, Rosie?' he asked, and the words that came off her tongue froze him dead.

'Your car.'

Daniel didn't speak as she lifted the page to show him, couldn't have if he wanted to. All of a sudden, he felt very faint.

'You alright there Daniel? Your jaw appears to have introduced itself to the floor.'

So transfixed was he by the page, he couldn't even tell if it was Keira or Amy who'd spoken to him.

'He's not going to get sick, is he?'

He might. The sweat that broke on his brow was just the first of his disbelieving body's reactions. His car. She'd drawn his car.

Mouth dry, Daniel put his finger on the page, right at the car's front. 'What are these?'

'Grass!' Rosanna exclaimed, glancing down at where he pointed to various squiggles of green and yellow, bustling from the illustrated turquoise hood. 'And leaves, and weeds, and, em, I don't have a name for this one, and *thorns*, and –'

'Where did you see these?' Daniel's head spun all over again, worse now than when he'd seen beneath the hood for real. Much worse.

'They broke your car,' Rosanna said simply, and pulled the sketchpad back to herself.

7

The forest was a strange place at night. In the absence of light it felt smaller, more closed in. Try and look at the sky above, and the view was blocked by a plethora of overhanging branches. The same ones that allowed golden sunlight to speckle in and dot the road did not allow for the pale moon's milky glow. The way ahead was darkness.

It was a moment before Daniel realised he wasn't alone. Probably because he never felt alone here, eyes were always on him, but this was different, not just eyes, a body. A small body. A familiar body.

Rosanna's dress appeared woven by the trees themselves, a short slip of vine and leaves, topped by a crown of reeds that saw blonde curls fall freely down her exposed shoulders. Her arms were totally bare, and though there was no light that should have allowed it, they seemed to glow, and lit the way ahead of them.

It was clear she was the lead, Daniel a mere disciple, and every now and then she'd pause in her gallop to glance back and laugh at him, though not in a nasty way. From the way the corners of his lips pulled ever upward, Daniel realised he must be laughing too. It had been so long since they'd come back, just the two of them, he forgot how happy it made her, how happy she made him, here.

'Come on,' the child called. 'We're almost there.'

They neared the end of the trees, but Rosanna didn't slow. Onward she plunged into the forest, beyond the forgotten road's final stone, and danced between the trees at will.

'Wait up!' Daniel called, though she'd slipped further forward. She may not be able to hear him. Little other choice, he sped after her, and as he too crossed the threshold past the final stone, the trees parted before him, marking a clear path to the girl, like Mozart and the red sea. *KAPOW!*

The deeper into the trees he ran, the more light began to creep through. Faint at first, but steadily growing, though not white like he'd expect, nor the golden rays of the sun. The light that filtered its way through was a thick green, and hazy. As he neared the end of the trees, it thickened to the point he almost lost sight of Rosanna, but at the last moment caught her dart out into a clearing.

The green was all around as he stepped out of the woods, a heavy fog. Above, the way to the sky was no longer blocked by branches, it lay open before them, but revealed nothing more than a sea of empty black. These thoughts were paltry, second-fiddle, to the sight that stood ahead.

In the middle of an otherwise empty field, a tree rose from the centre of a circular embankment. The fort itself was impressive enough, rising some two metres from the ground, but it paled in comparison to that mighty tree. It defied description. Defied classification. It was neither birch, nor ash, nor alder, yet somehow all of them, together. It touched the clouds and beyond, higher than Daniel could lift his head to see, thicker than his and Keira's car combined. Here it stood, in the middle of the clearing, untouched by time, *older* than time, just like the stories.

Rosanna stood at its base, marvelling up at the behemoth in much the same way Daniel had, only where he was frozen rigid to the spot, she leapt forward and clung to its bark. Daniel almost started forward, thinking with nothing to cling to, she'd fall in an instant, and hard. But with each raise of a hand, her little fingers found nests and handholds in the ancient being's many knots and weathers.

Daniel did move then, if she could climb it, then he could do the same, and maybe the secrets behind all this would finally be revealed, finally put to right, but a voice from behind stopped him dead in his tracks.

'Daniel?'

He whirled around, suddenly back on the famine road, the tree and its mysterious green fog vanished from sight, all things vanished, shrouded in darkness once more, but for the endless stones that stretched on in either direction, and his wife, Keira, naked, and staring, but not at him.

Daniel followed her shell-shocked gaze to where it landed on her exposed legs, which ran dark and wet and violent. She brought a hand to the mess and it came away soaked red, as the crimson river flowed ceaselessly, terminally down from her crotch to the ground, to form a darkened pool on the cold stones below.

'Daniel?' she croaked.

But he was already gone.

*

Daniel woke to a chill breeze, billowing its way in through his open bedroom door, and shivered. The next thing he noticed besides the cold was the sickly stink of sweat, and his skin recoiled as he pulled clinging damp cotton over his shoulders, leaving him colder still as he set out for the kitchen.

The dreams were coming more or less every night now. They weren't always the same, sometimes his dad was there at the end of the clearing, sometimes other voices called to him besides Keira, but they always ended that way, with her, and the blood.

The enchanting scent of freshly fried cured meat called to him, but not before he stopped to see the front door lay open.

'Keira, you out there?'

'In here,' came the call from the kitchen.

'Front door's open.'

'Oh.'

Daniel grumbled to himself about heating bills that he wasn't sure he even paid as he shut out the breeze and slipped into the kitchen, shivering still.

'Rashers and sausages?' Keira asked from the hob.

'Sure, sounds good yeah,' Daniel said, hugging his arms tight to his chest. 'Christ I'm freezing.'

Keira turned to look at him and snorted, covering her mouth with a spatula. 'Well maybe if you weren't running around buck-arse naked, put some clothes on for God's sake.'

'Got another one of those under-armours I can borrow?'

'Where's this newfound fascination for my clothes coming from? You're not becoming a cross-dresser are you?'

'And what if I was? Would you leave me if – Hey!' Daniel flinched as a slice of black pudding caught him just below the right nipple.

'Come back when you've put some clothes on,' Keira said, launching another cut of meat. 'You're indecent.'

Daniel caught the rebound of pudding against his chest and wedged it between his teeth á la Corleone, gave Keira a great beaming smile before he was summarily hounded out of the kitchen with the paddling utensil.

Suitably clothed, Daniel re-emerged from his bedroom to collect the rest of his breakfast, and stopped again. The door was open, again.

'Keira?'

'You better not be wearing any of my nice skirts, you'll stretch them out,' came the muted reply.

Daniel swallowed. 'Rosanna?'

'Yeah?'

Daniel poked his head into her room to see her lying on her bed, hunched over her latest drawing. Whatever it was, he didn't care to look at it.

'Everything okay?' he asked.

Rosanna's face became a pout. 'The nibs keep breaking.'

'Oh,' Daniel said, and watched how she gripped the pencil, firmly clasped around all four fingers and pointed downwards, like one might a dagger. 'Well maybe don't press them against the page so hard.'

'Have to.'

'Okay.' A fresh breeze blew in through the open doorway. 'You didn't open the front door, did you Rosie?'

Rosanna shook her head. 'Can you get me the crayons? They won't break so easy.'

Daniel looked around the room, but between all the boxes of books, toys and teddies, he hadn't a clue where to begin. 'Sure, where are they?'

'In the shed.'

'In the shed?'

Rosanna nodded.

'Why are they in the shed?'

She shrugged. 'That's where you put them.'

Daniel stared at her. 'What?'

Rosanna glanced up from her drawing. 'That's where you put them, after I showed you your car, remember?'

Daniel's heartbeat quickened, and his saliva dried out. He certainly did not remember. 'When was this?'

'After we went to Amy's. After bed time, when you came in, remember?'

'No,' Daniel whispered. The colour was draining out of him. 'Wh-why did I say I was taking them?'

'You didn't. You just said "these go in the shed now" and then you left. I didn't really mind cos I like the pencils more anyway but now they keep breaking, so can you get me the crayons back?'

'Yeah, yeah sure,' Daniel said, wondering how he was going to make it to the shed and back without falling over. 'Just, um, just don't mention about the crayons to your mother, okay?'

'Okay,' Rosanna said, and turned back to her paper.

Outside, the fresh air did nothing to salve his flaming lungs. When? And how? Had he been sleepwalking again? Had it really gotten to this extent? His mind raced and ran and rushed and rattled, but through it all there was one overriding thought. Stephen. Stephen, and not-Stephen. What if the person Rosanna had seen hadn't been Daniel? Had been not-Daniel? She was part of this, somehow. Keira wasn't, but she was. Why?

As he stumbled towards the shed, he began to notice little drops of red in the gravel, and slowed. Turning to face the way he'd come, he saw they stretched back past the front door, and beyond to the driveway. It wasn't blood, he wouldn't allow himself to believe it was blood, but even so his chest tightened, and another shiver tore through him. Blood or no, there wasn't a chance he was following them down there.

Maybe it was paint. Highly unlikely, but as the droplets continued all the way to the shed's door, he was willing to believe anything. He reached for the handle, and slowly let his wrist fall away. The lock, the one he'd put up after Rosanna had given herself a paint-job, was gone. The door hung open, and the drops continued on inside. Goosebumps rose, Daniel threw a glance over his shoulder to check he wasn't being watched, and followed them in.

It was darker in the shed than it should have been, and Daniel immediately saw the cause. The little window at the back of the building was completely shattered, yet somehow still hung in place. The glass had split in an almost cobweb pattern, and the result was that it showered the dusty wooden interior with incredible spiralling shadows.

On a chipped table to his left sat Rosanna's crayons, sprawled in a massive heap atop a couple of her sketchpads. She hadn't mentioned him taking them too, if indeed it had been him. Daniel prayed that it was, but he left them where they sat for the moment, eyes drawn to the floor again. The little red drops led all the way to the cracked window.

Daniel floated towards the light source, a twisting circle pulling him in, until his hand came to hover just shy of the window's centre, to the thing that had caused it to fragment. It couldn't be.

One half hung limply this side of the shattered glass, while the other protruded proudly out, flapping like a sail in the wind. A sail with a red stain right at its tip.

Daniel brushed his thumb against the blade of grass, the same one he'd pulled from the entrails of his recently deceased goldfish, the very same he'd lain at the foot of his long dead grandmother's grave, and the moment his skin met with the grass, that was it. They were fused.

Daniel stared dumbly at his thumb, a length of green sticking out the end of it, no indication of an entry point, just a simple extension of his flesh. Shock lasted only a couple of motionless seconds, before fear kicked in and he yanked backwards. Rather than free himself from the intwination, the window exploded inward, pelted him with glass.

He stumbled back unharmed, eyes glued to his thumb, thumb glued to the errant blade. He pinched, squeezed, pulled, yanked, tore, but it wouldn't come loose, and what was worse, each tug sent a tremendous, searing pain right through his nervous system. Frantic, his gaze darted about the shed. There had to something, scissors, shears, a chainsaw, anything to get this… this *thing* off him. As his eyes bounced from one empty shelf to another, however, they landed instead on the pile of Rosanna's crayons, and the open sketchpad beneath.

Daniel's blood went cold. Had it been open before? That didn't matter, it was open now, and Rosanna's latest drawing stared back at him, bright and green and vibrant. Daniel stepped forward,

155

and it was like looking at his reflection, only a real mirror image this time, the mirror of what he felt, that which could not be seen.

On the page, a child's rendition of a man, and everything that was wrong with him. Little squiggles of green poked out from the nose, marking strings of grass much like the one imbued in Daniel's hand. Meanwhile, the arms weren't arms at all, but tree branches, straight and stiff and sideways. Creeping vine wrapped its way around the legs, choked them as they dug beneath cloth and flesh, where they finally met toes of gangrenous swollen mush. In the bottom corner of the page, scrawled in Rosanna's signature, barely-legible script, was one word.

'DADDY.'

6

A closed door was a safe door. As long as Daniel stood out in the hall, Rosanna's crayons in a box under one arm, her sketchpad in the other, he would continue to be safe. The two of them would continue to be safe. The moment that door opened, and he stepped inside her room, this might no longer be the case.

'Daniel are you eating these or not? It's getting cold.'

Keira's call from the kitchen made him jump, and reminded him that he could not stay here forever, eternally playing the dweller-on-the-threshold. This was no dream, much as he might like otherwise.

156

'Yeah, two seconds I'm just helping Rosanna with something.'

The door was closed. Daniel's fingers twitched over the handle. The door was safe. The door was –

Open.

Rosanna stood at the entrance to her room, hands on hips. 'Did you get them?'

Without answering, Daniel stepped inside. He set the crayons down on her desk beside a pile of broken nibs, and as she moved to inspect, held a hand up to stall her.

'Rosie…' he said softly, suddenly aware of just how fast his heart was thumping. 'I wanted to ask you about this.'

Rosanna's face slipped from quiet indignation at being denied access to her colours to simple curiosity as she approached the page Daniel held out for her. With wrung hands she studied it, like an art critic far beyond her years, before turning that analytical gaze on him.

'Don't you like it?'

Daniel looked from the child to the drawing, and back again. Never before had he been so aware of clothes on skin, pulling him, weighing him down. 'I… I think it's very good, Rosie. What is it about, do you mind if I ask?'

Rosanna's face crinkled in mild confusion. 'What do you mean?'

'These squiggles, coming out of the face, and the long brown arms, what are they?'

Rosanna shrugged. 'Just something I dreamed.'

'Something you dreamed?' Daniel asked, as his eyes darted to his thumb where the blade of grass protruded, and quickly tucked it behind the pad. 'Not anything you've seen for real?'

Rosanna merely frowned at him.

'What kind of dream was it, Rosie? Do you have them often?'

The frown deepened to a pout, and Rosanna reached past him to grab a handful of crayons. 'Don't wanna talk about those dreams.'

Daniel swallowed as she sat cross-legged on the floor before her latest creation, a simple doodle of a beach. 'Why not?'

Ignoring Daniel's earlier advice, Rosanna took hold of the blue crayon in a vice-grip as her brows clouded over, and ground it into the page. 'Bad dreams.'

Daniel tried to wet his tongue, but found no saliva. 'You know you can tell me about them, if you like?'

Rosanna looked up briefly from her page, and eyed him with something approaching suspicion. 'Don't want to.'

'You don't want to talk about them at all, or you don't want to talk to me?'

Rosanna didn't answer, her attention was solely on the drawing beneath her now.

Daniel turned the one in his hands back towards him. What did it mean? Did she know? She had to know, first the car, and now this, it couldn't be coincidence. Could it?

'Does something bad happen in the dream?'

158

Rosanna paused, only for a moment, and then without looking up, nodded.

'Does something bad happen to Daddy?'

Another pause, longer this time, followed by a slow shake of the head.

Rather than relief, confusion flooded him. He thought of his own dreams, of Keira, and his heart faltered. 'Does something bad happen to Mum?'

Rosanna looked up, met him with a narrow gaze, and shook her head again. Beneath the orange blaze of her eyes, Daniel had never felt so cold.

'What, then?'

Rosanna's lips bunched together, and she turned back to the drawing, pressing the blue crayon deeper into the sheet with renewed vigour. It was only then Daniel saw her eyes were blurred.

'What is it, Rosie? Why are you upset?'

She didn't respond, gripped the crayon tighter, pressed it harder, barely even moving it anymore, just pinned it down as far into the page as it would go, and then it snapped. Rosanna stared at the bisected object in her palm as a new colour bloomed. Where the crayon broke in two, with such force had the split occurred that the top-end piece dug into her skin, and blood bubbled down to her wrist.

'Jesus, Rosanna, let me see –' Daniel began, but was cut short by her shriek.

'Don't touch me!'

Daniel fell back in horror as the child shuffled away from him, pressed herself against the far wall as she started to rock back and forth, and sob.

'It's *me*,' Rosanna managed to squeak between her tears. She held up her bloodied hand for all the world to see. 'I'm the one who gets hurt.'

5

The gate was shut. The old frayed rope that held it firm had been returned. Where it had gone, who had taken it, no longer concerned Daniel. Coasting off the adrenaline that had seen him leave Rosanna's room and head straight down the road, he vaulted over the fence in one fluid motion.

Eyes on him. That was the immediate feeling. It always was, here, he'd just gotten so used to suppressing it that he told himself it wasn't real, but there was no mistaking that sensation. Raised hackles, distant thoughts of sweat, unease. They weren't important. If there were eyes on him, then someone, or some*thing*, was watching, and it was beyond time to find out who.

'What do you want with her?'

Sharp, hoarse, riddled with emotion, the only answer a gentle sigh on the breeze.

'Why are you doing this? What have I ever done to you? What has *she* ever done to you?'

160

Stones bounced and rolled beneath Daniel's feet as he marched deeper into the forest, kicking up plumes of chalky dust.

'I never did anything to offend you. I've never harmed your trees or your floor, so what do you want?'

Daniel was aware of how he must have looked, a weary, pale-faced man with lines beyond his years yelling at some swaying trees, but he didn't care. If there was no-one out here, then he could yell and scream and piss and shout as much as he liked, and it wouldn't make a difference, but if those eyes were real…

'You took my parents,' Daniel said, pausing to stare at the dented tree. 'Isn't that enough? Is he here, still? Dad? Dad are you out here?'

An increase in gale, a slight rustling of branches, but that was all. Daniel held up his thumb for the whole forest to see, as the grass at its tip fluttered in the breeze.

'Is this what you did to him?' Daniel pictured the shrubs in his father's beard, the mesh of nettles that clung to his hair. He thought of the sap. 'Am I going to end up like that, too? Is she?'

Bitter tears stung his eyes as he spun around in a circle, looking for a glimpse of something, anything, to tell him he wasn't just a madman standing at the end of an empty abandoned road. 'What do you want from –'

His words fell short, as his eyes landed on something new at last. Not new, he corrected himself, in a daze. Missing.

Daniel counted the trees that lined the way down from this end of the road. One, two, three, gap, four. That was how it went. He turned to the other side, and counted the same length down. One, two, three, four, five. No gap. Back to the nearside. One, two, three, *gap*, five. That was how it really went.

'So you're saying that there used to be a tree-sprout here, and now there's a tree. Fascinating stuff Daniel, really.'

Keira's voice was a message from the ancient past. The fourth tree, the one he'd been so pleased with himself to find, was gone. Not felled, there was no stump, nor uprooted, simply gone. How?

'Daniel.'

If Keira's melodic murmur had been from the ancient past, then the croaked husk that sent ripples through Daniel's eardrums and froze him solid was prehistoric. Frozen solid in the literal sense. As footsteps crunched in the stones behind him and his heart threatened to burst through its ribcage, Daniel was pinned in place, as if this were one of his dreams.

The footsteps moved round to his front, and unable to bend his neck, Daniel's eyes followed them up, and landed on a sick mockery of his father.

Martin Cawley had died in that car accident. What stood before Daniel now was the result of a long and grotesque surgery, the only tools those of which were at the forest's disposal. Splintered bone protruded from a broken neck, which barely held a concave head in place via a scarf of ivy that stitched its way through mottled flesh. Where his chest had been obliterated by the impact of the crash, bark poked through the punctures left behind, maintaining the shape of his torso. All the clothes he'd worn before, the shabby cloak and battered boots, they were gone now, but he didn't appear naked. What little flesh there was on view was seen through a coat of leaves and bracken, woven together by thorny brambles that dug into bone and sinew, lacerating skin that leaked golden syrup. Sap.

'I'm sorry you have to see me like this,' Daniel's father croaked, and without wanting to, he found their gazes locked.

The eyes were perhaps the worst of all. Beneath their milky surface, maggots writhed and burrowed, feasting upon a bottomless pupil. Countless disappeared inside that endless black, while more reappeared at the edge of his sockets, starting the ceaseless stream again.

'And I'm sorry for the position this puts you in.'

If Daniel could have flinched at the stench that open mouth brought, he would have. Tongue, like eyeballs, were infested with larvae. They'd chewed almost entirely through gum and taste-buds both. The teeth they must have taken care of long ago, whatever pearly-whites Daniel had seen in those wedding photos had been replaced by small jagged wood, tiny little branches, and the skin on his lips was scabbed over with bark. The smell was toxic. Rot and disease reeked from every word.

'It's the only way I can speak and be sure you won't try run away.'

Realisation dawned, and Daniel's eyes bulged. *He* was pinning him here like this. Somehow, some way, his father had paralysed him.

163

'There's something I need to tell you,' Martin Cawley said. 'Something I fear you may already know.'

Daniel tried to shake his head, couldn't.

'They're angry at you Daniel. You took something from them and now they want it back.'

What was he talking about? He hadn't taken anything! Never so much as a stone or a tree branch, he knew better than that. *Feared* better than that.

'You're resisting it, I can see that, but you know. You know what you've taken.'

Daniel's head twitched the slightest increment in denial.

'She's not yours Daniel.'

Daniel closed his eyes. He would not listen to this – would not! – but his father's words crept into his ears just the same.

'She's no more your daughter than you are my son.'

For a moment, Daniel kept them closed, as the crystal clear forest air filled his lungs, and the reverberation of a broken voice made him weak at the knees.

'She was conceived here,' Martin went on, 'As were you, as was I. It calls to us, this place. The men in our family, it calls to us, ever since your great-great-grandfather struck that deal with them. We cannot escape it, and we doom those around us as a result. *They* call to us.'

Who? Daniel wanted to ask, but he already knew the answer. As for this "deal", Granny Cawley had never mentioned anything about that.

'I tried to fight it, but I couldn't. You've seen it, you've felt it. Life here, it's like no place else. It's open and pure and *free*. It... reacts with us, like a chemical. Your mother became pregnant with you because of what we did in these woods, because of that chemical, because of that *life*. To them, that's as much a right to ownership as if they'd gotten her pregnant themselves.'

Daniel could only blink. Even if he could speak now, he wouldn't have a word to say.

'Do you know what a changeling is, Daniel? A changeling is a child that has been replaced by a faery. Rosanna is not a changeling, she has not been replaced, because she was never yours in the first place. This is their ground, those that are conceived here belong to them. The only thing that will make them forgo that ownership is if you give them something else in return.'

Martin paused, and Daniel saw miniscule droplets of sap had begun to leak from the edges of his maggot-laden eyes.

'I loved you, Daniel. You may not remember that, but I did, more than anything. I tried to save you, and it cost me *everything*. My life, your mother's life, and the life of our unborn child. I thought they could be reasoned with, bargained. I thought they might take me, and leave them untouched. They don't want to be reasoned with, Daniel, they can't be. They want what they want, and if they can't get it, they'll take something else.

'You can save yourself from the same fate as me. If you give Rosanna back to them, you and Keira can both live on with your new child, your own child. Neither of you have to die. You can be happy, and not… like me.'

Martin let out a long, shuddering breath, and his body signalled a chorus of creaks and groans as he turned to look beyond where the famine road ended. Far enough that way, and there'd be a clearing. And then, a fort, and a tree. Martin turned that horrid gaze back on Daniel. 'You know what you have to do.'

Like an anvil hoisted from his chest, Daniel found he could breathe again. Could talk.

'What would happen to her?' he croaked.

'They'd take her in,' Martin said. 'As one of their own, not like me. They'd raise her, here, amongst the trees. She'd like it, really. You've seen what she's like here.'

'And… and Keira? Amy, Mary, Stephen, Joe, Sam? School, Social Services? What will they all say when she goes missing? When she disappears? It would break her, Keira, it… it would break me.'

Martin looked at Daniel levelly. The sap around his eyes was gone. 'You don't understand, do you Daniel? They can make it so that *she never was*. Think of all the unbelievable things that have happened in the past few weeks that only you have been able to see. Only you and her that is, though she hasn't reached full viewing yet. If they can do that, if they can hide that from everyone but you, then think of what else they can do, of the things they can make people *unsee*. Every trace of her, every record, every memory, they'll all be gone by the time the dust has settled. But know this Daniel, you have to make sure the dust settles. Don't do what I did, don't shirk your responsibility to your family. Do what you must, and ensure that it is done. There's not much time left.'

Three lives, or one. He stared at the father who was not. A family, or this.

'What about me?' Daniel's voice was a tremor. 'Will I remember?'

Martin only returned the gaze, saying nothing.

Daniel swallowed, looked away. 'How much time?'

'New Year's,' Martin said. 'Your true child will have a heartbeat by then, and at that stage, it will be too late. Once they know you've created life without first giving back what is theirs, then they will take it from you, like they did from me.'

New Year's. Not even ten days. He wanted to deny it, to refuse, but he remembered the sheet of newspaper that brought him here so recently. He remembered the headline. He knew the truth of his mother's death.

'Will they leave me alone, then? Will they leave us alone?'

Martin nodded. 'Your new family will be free from this curse. Once you've done what you must, go. Get out of here, as far away as you can, so that the men of our line will never have to deal with this again.'

New Year's, Daniel thought, and shivered. 'You mentioned a deal, one my great-great-grandfather struck. What deal? I thought the faeries let him go so he would tell the story of what happened.'

Martin shook his head. 'I've said enough for now. Too much. If they believe I've overstepped my lines, the punishment will be great. I'm sorry, Daniel, truly.'

Daniel blinked, and the gap between the trees was gone. So too was his father. In his place, the fourth tree was returned. In tiny streaking runnels, little bits of sap coursed down its bark.

He understood now. Rosanna's drawing, the grass in his hand, the moss. He knew what awaited him, if he did not do his duty. He thought of the headline once more, and knew what awaited Keira, too. New Year's.

Nine days, to see that it was done.

4

The kitchen door swung open the moment Daniel stepped inside the house, and Keira stormed out to meet him.

'What the fuck?'

Daniel didn't have time to open his mouth.

'Where were you?'

Keira's eyes bore holes in his skull, demanding an answer, her forehead creased with furious worry.

'I... I was...' Daniel had no idea what to say. He barely had an idea of where he was, the walk home a hazy splash in his memory. All he could think of was New Year's.

'You disappear for an hour without telling me where you've gone, without a phone, with no way of contacting you, and then you just stroll back in without even preparing an excuse?' In the battle between fury and worry, there was starting to look like only one winner. 'What the fuck is wrong with you? What makes you think it's okay to keep doing that?'

'I…' words failed him. He couldn't explain, couldn't begin to explain. Though she stood right in front of him, red-eyed and shaking, all he could picture was her naked, and the blood that flowed ceaselessly down her legs.

'That's twice, Daniel. Twice. Two times, you've scared me absolutely out of my mind. What do you expect me to do when I look all over the house and you're gone without a trace? When Rosanna's crying her eyes out, her hand covered in blood, and what the hell was that about anyway? Do you know?'

Daniel's lips moved, but no sound came forth. Was he even here now? After everything he'd just seen, somehow this was what felt surreal. Distantly, he heard himself speak at last. 'She… she snapped a crayon and it cut into her.'

If Keira's eyes had bored before, they positively drilled now. 'So you saw that had happened, and you just left her?'

'She… told me not to touch her.'

She was going to punch him, she was going to punch him right in the face, he could see it in her eyes, just how much she wanted to.

'She told you not to touch her?' Keira whispered. 'She's your *daughter*, Daniel. I mean what the –' she couldn't finish the sentence, only stood and stared.

Daniel stepped forward, a hesitant arm reaching for hers. 'Keira, I –'

'Don't. You're not allowed touch me, not until you tell me where you were.'

Whether he wanted to or not, Daniel found himself staring into her eyes. Her beautiful, furious, burning blue eyes. He couldn't tell her. His father had told his mother, and look where that had gotten them.

'Nothing?' Keira asked, and her voice wobbled. 'You're not going to tell me anything? What's wrong with you? Why are you doing this to me?'

Daniel brushed for her arm again. 'Keira –'

'Fuck off.' She batted it away. 'Just fuck off. I can't believe –' she paused to let out a shaky breath. 'Rosanna! Rosanna get in the car.'

That snapped Daniel into gear. 'What do you mean? Where are you taking her?'

Keira's eyes bulged. 'Oh, so now you suddenly care? Tell me where you've been and I'll tell you where I'm going.'

The kitchen door opened and Rosanna stepped out, a bandage wrapped around her palm. Daniel's gaze flicked between them as sweat began to trickle, but his mouth stayed shut.

Keira met that gaze, and shook her head in slow horror. 'What's the matter with you?'

She moved to walk past him and before he could stop himself Daniel's arm shot out and grasped hers, panic overriding thought. If Keira left with Rosanna, who knew how long she'd be gone, or where she was going? What if she went to Meath, to her parents, and he left here without a car? What if New Year's came and went, and him not there to... to...

'Let go of me! Let go of me now!'

Daniel blinked, glanced down and saw the flesh on her arm was purpling around his fingers. Immediately he released the grip, stunned.

Keira stared at her arm, then back at Daniel, her mouth hanging open, as if seeing him for the first time. 'Who are you?'

From the kitchen doorway, Rosanna watched it all. Daniel swallowed. A criminal in his own home.

'This, this is your last chance, Daniel,' Keira spoke, but his eyes were only for the child. 'Where were you?'

Daniel looked at Rosanna, and Rosanna looked back at him.

'The road,' he said at last. 'I went down to the road.'

'The road.' Keira repeated, and Daniel nodded. 'Well if you love that road so much, why don't you just fucking stay there?'

She was past him in an instant, with Rosanna close behind. Daniel didn't move as the car engine flickered to life behind him, didn't flinch as its wheels tore out the driveway, stranding him here.

All he did was stand alone in the empty hallway, stand and stare, and, after a little while, slump, and another while after that, cry.

*

The alcohol didn't numb, it couldn't, Daniel was numb already. What it did do was provide warmth, and in this he was sorely lacking. He glanced up at the clock but its mysteries remained hidden by hands that swayed interminably. That it was dark outside was enough to show Keira had been gone for hours. Keira, and Rosanna.

He could not call her, after his phone's battery had exploded he'd still yet to get a new one, and the landline hadn't worked this side of the millennium. He had no idea where she was, how long she'd be, or indeed if she was ever coming back. So this was what it felt like. Utter fucking hell.

Daniel refilled his glass, the Jameson bottle two-thirds of the way spent. What was his endgame, here, if she didn't come back soon? Return to the forest and beg? He couldn't foresee that going well. Walk to town, find a payphone and try call her? And what if she didn't pick up? Run away?

Daniel rolled up his shirtsleeve, studied the hardened skin of his arms. Just beneath the surface, where veins should course, he saw none, only the faint hint of something solid, something dappled, something wooden. Running away was not an option.

And if she did come back – which, surely she had to, it was three days to Christmas, for God's sake – what then? Would he do as his father, the bloody tree-person, had said? Could he?

He leant his head back against the couch, and stared at the kitchen ceiling. There weren't any water-stains in here, no smiling faces, yet voices swirled in his head just the same.

It's like you're scared of her.

Do you think she is your daughter?

Not scared in that way.

Of course she's not yours. How could she be yours?

She's no more your daughter than you are my son.

It's me. I'm the one who gets hurt.

She's beautiful.

Scared that she might hurt you.

She's perfect.

Who knew how long he might have lain there, eyes closed, tormented by the incorporeal? All night, perhaps, if he'd only drifted off a minute or two earlier. As it was, the drink did not quite have him in its throes enough to blot out the sound of a knock at the door.

Daniel's eyes shot open. *Keira.* He was on his feet and into the hallway before he'd given things a second thought, which, seeing the silhouette of a figure through the frosted glass window, he did now. Eyes on the mystery visitor, Daniel's steps slowed. Keira wouldn't knock, this was her home, she'd simply walk in. Besides, from the outline, it didn't look like a woman.

Perhaps it was Joe, maybe Keira had phoned him and told him what happened, asked if he'd go check on him, make sure he was alright. Perhaps, but the closer Daniel got to the door, the less likely this seemed. Joe was impatient. He wouldn't hang around, as this person did now, he probably wouldn't have even knocked either, just barged on in. The door wasn't locked, after all.

Slightly uneasy and suddenly chilled again, the whiskey's warmth a distant embrace, Daniel reached for the handle, saw the silhouette take a small step back to accommodate him, and pushed open the door.

On the front step, stood nothing. Empty. Blank. Devoid. No-one. Daniel's breath did not come easy as he peered around the driveway. No movement, no sound, no signs of disturbance. Nothing.

Slowly, Daniel closed the door. No sooner had he done so than two raps sounded out, made him leap on the spot, synapses firing, and when he looked back at the frosted window, the figure had returned.

Daniel swallowed. 'Who's there?'

For an answer, he received two more raps on the door. Throughout, the figure remained perfectly still.

Already cold, Daniel shuddered. How could it knock without moving a muscle?

'I said who is it?' Daniel demanded with a bravado he did not feel.

Silence met him, no knock, but the silhouette remained. Daniel's hand flicked up to the lock and snapped it shut. Without ever taking his eyes from the figure, he backed down the hallway, all the way to the kitchen, and propped the door open with a chair. Still unblinking, he edged to the utensil drawer, and slid it open behind his back.

The figure didn't budge.

Daniel felt around for the steak knife, and felt a brief tingle as the blade of grass in his thumb brushed against its sharp edge. Cutting it out would be beyond pain, he knew, but he didn't have time to think on that now. Fingers rested on the knife hilt, and Daniel picked it up.

THUD-THUD.

Despite having never looked away Daniel still jumped at this latest knock, and nearly dropped the knife. He let out a shaky breath. It was totally unnerving, seeing that figure completely unmoved, while the door shook in its frame. He reaffirmed his grip on the handle and, holding the knife straight out in front of him, inched towards the front door again.

But for a slight spinning in his head, he felt almost entirely sober now. Sweat prickled his armpits in spite of the cold and his hands were clammy on the knife's grip. He could feel it watching him. Waiting for him.

'Who is it?' It was a plea, more than anything. Please tell me who you are. Please let me put this away. Please, just, leave me alone.

No response, and no movement either. Watching. Waiting.

The handle was slick beneath Daniel's sweaty palms as he undid the lock. A closed door was a safe door. Daniel opened it, and stepped back, breathless.

There was no-one there.

Daniel's breath poured out in relieved gasps, almost to the point of hyperventilating. That was when he saw it. Movement from outside, a white blur in the deep of night, there one moment, gone the next. Before he knew what he was doing, Daniel had rushed out after it, screaming.

'Leave me alone! Get away from here! Just leave me fucking be!'

Tears stung at his eyes as the cold whipped his flesh and the gravel dug into his feet, waiting for a response he knew he'd never get. Why couldn't they just leave him be?

Daniel stared out into the night for a moment longer as his racing heart gradually slowed, stared down the road to the forest where it would eventually lead, and squinted for a glimpse of something, anything, some life amidst all that shadow. He got none. There was only the cold.

Until he turned around.

Hallucinations were something countless years of night terrors had made Daniel accustomed to. That was how he knew that what stood in front of him was not one of them.

His house had two front doors.

Side by side, set into the white brick structure, they stood as if they belonged, watching him, like he was the weird one. The door on the left, the door which had always been there, looked, in as much as it could, normal. Just beside it, on the right, a mirror image, each of its features flipped. Handle on the right when it should be left, diagonal slant pointed in the opposite direction, even chips in the paint did not escape the redesign. What chilled Daniel most were not these minute discrepancies, however, it was something far more simple than that. On the left, through the glass frame in the real door, the hallway light was on. On the right, darkness.

'What is this?' Daniel whispered, and, for answer, the door on the right creaked open.

Daniel looked around, but there was no-one else here. The spectral figure was gone, leaving this in its wake.

Knowing he shouldn't, that he should just slip back through into the comfort of a lighted hallway and the last of his Jameson, knowing it was madness, he walked to the imposter door.

It blew open left to right, and Daniel stepped inside.

Drunk, dark, and absolutely terrified, his disorientation was complete. The mirroring had not stopped with the door. Swaying on the step, Daniel took in this mockery of his home, and tried to get his bearings. Rosanna's room, the bathroom, the fork in the hallway that led to his and Keira's room, they were all on the wrong side. It was worse than wrong, it was sickening. The house he'd lived in all his life, and they'd made this of it. Why?

177

As Daniel took another step into the funhouse, he heard a sound. A rustle. He raised the knife he hadn't realised he was still holding as his eyes darted about to see where it came from, and, landing on a small crack in the plaster wall, he saw it.

Brambles, burrowing their way from the inside out. Daniel could only gawp as flecks of paint fell to the carpet, and leapt when he saw that too underwent changes of its own. Dandelions, thistles, daisies, each sprung up from indistinguishable tears in the seams, and even as he stared another *crack* to his left made him jump again, like a startled rabbit. Nettles poured out from the skirting boards, wriggling up the walls where they intersected with thorny branches, and drew his eyes up towards the ceiling, where the lightbulb had burst outwards, the source of disseminating vines. They spread across the hallway in all directions, and blocked the path forward.

Locked in place, Daniel's jaw dropped at the realisation that the ceaseless growth was not aimless. The brambles, the nettles, the thistles and vines, each had a specific destination in mind. Photos. Family photos that lined the walls.

He, Keira and Rosanna, down at Ballyfarreg beach on a sunny afternoon. Rosanna had built a sandcastle, her first, and the three of them stood proudly over it. Noiseless, a rip in the picture appeared, emanating from behind. Twisting thorns poked their way through the sandcastle and wrapped their way around Rosanna's neck, continued until her face disappeared too, and finally, her body. After that, they simply stopped moving. He and Keira were left untouched.

178

Suddenly nauseous, Daniel stumbled back from the photo, holding his mouth, and frantically glanced around to see the pattern repeated itself with every last one of the pictures. He and Keira, happy and smiling. Rosanna, utterly destroyed.

'No,' Daniel said. 'No.'

This was how they'd do it. First the photos, then the memories themselves. Of Rosanna there'd be nothing left at all.

'No.'

It was too much. Too brutal. Relentless. He couldn't do it.

Rosanna's first day of school, posing in her uniform in front of the fireplace, reduced to a photo of the empty hearth. Rosanna kicking a football in the garden. Only the ball remained. Opening her Christmas stocking beneath the tree. Gone.

'No!'

Daniel turned and ran for the door, but tripped on the brambles that hampered his way as it started to swing slowly shut in front of him. The vines that fell from the ceiling thickened, consolidated, and found a new target. Daniel batted away stem and branch with the useless steak knife as he tried and failed to rise to his feet. There was no stopping them, they were too many and too strong, endless. Thorns wrapped around his neck as nettles blistered skin, cutting him, choking him, pinning him down. There had to be some way out, had to, but Daniel couldn't see it, couldn't see anything but the branches and the blood and Rosanna. He couldn't die here, not like this, not now, but the door was closing and the grip was tightening and Daniel couldn't move, couldn't breathe, couldn't scream, and then the vines were inside him, they sprawled down his throat as brambles ripped flesh, wrapped around bone, and as the dim light of the moon finally winked out, and the front door slammed shut, pain consumed him, and he was gone.

3

'Daniel? Daniel! Jesus Christ… Rosanna go to your room.'

The noises didn't wake him, because he hadn't been asleep. For a while there, he simply wasn't. Now, it seemed, by degrees, he was slowly coming back to himself. A toe in the ribs sped the process along.

'Get up,' Keira said, as he flinched from the prod. 'And clean up. I'll be in the kitchen.'

Daniel's crusted eyes peeled their way open, just in time to see Keira's heels turn tail and disappear into the other room. He lifted his head, which came up wet and sticky. On the floor, a pile of vomit larger than himself made for his pillow. Daniel wiped the chunks from his face and moved to a seated position, head pounding.

Where…? And how…?

The last thing he remembered were vines and brambles pouring down his throat, slicing him apart from the inside out. He rubbed at his Adam's apple, the only remnant of anything wrong an overwhelming thirst.

'What are you doing?'

Daniel's head snapped round to where Rosanna stood in the doorway of her room, and his heart plummeted. He restrained himself from the urge to glance at the photos that lined the wall, but fear gnawed him regardless.

'Just having a rest,' he croaked. 'My head was sore and I needed a lie down.'

Rosanna pursed her lips. The big cloth bandage that wrapped her hand when last he saw her had been replaced by a simple plaster. Strangely, it was his hand she seemed interested in. 'What happened to your hand? That looks sore too.'

Daniel's gaze flicked down to the tiny green blade that stuck from his thumb, and his eyes widened. 'Can you see –'

'Rosanna! I said go to your room. Get away from that puke before you get sick.'

At her mother's charge, Rosanna quickly did as she was told. Daniel's head continued to thump as he swung it round to Keira. She pointed at the vomit.

'Clean that up, and clean yourself up. It's fucking Christmas, for God's sake.'

Before he could respond, she disappeared into the kitchen again, leaving Daniel to stare after her, slack-jawed. Christmas? Christmas Eve? Christmas *Day*? Neither could be right. Yesterday was the 22nd. It couldn't be. It didn't make any sense. Daniel glanced back down at the pile of sick, which only last night had been a pile of thistles and thorns, in a house that mirrored this one. Sense did not apply.

Confused and shivering, he pulled himself from the floor and into the bathroom, where he painstakingly removed his puke-stained shirt. He felt weaker than he ever had in his life, which would make sense if, on top of everything else, he'd now gone at least twenty-four hours without food or drink. Once he'd piled what much of the vomit he could into toilet tissues and flushed them away, he poured some carpet cleaner on what remained and shuffled into the kitchen.

'Forgetting for a minute what I just saw,' Keira began before the door had even closed behind him, her face bristling red, 'and the fact that I was *this* close to leaving you here to wallow alone, it's Christmas, and for her sake I can't bloody well spend it in a house she doesn't know.'

Daniel opened his mouth to speak, but she overrode him.

'That does *not* mean I've forgiven you. In fact, if anything coming back and seeing what you've been up to in our absence has made me quite a bit more fucking livid, but we're a family and as much as you're a stupid, egotistic, self-serving dickhead, I love you and I don't want to do it without you. Maybe I overreacted a little bit, leaving like that, but you *scared* me, Daniel, and so soon after what happened before. You have to know better, you have to. You promised me you'd look after me, that things would be different, but if you're already like this… You can't keep doing this to me. I can't take it.'

She was right, too, he could see it in the lines across her forehead, in the bags under her swollen red eyes. She couldn't take it anymore than he could.

'I'm sorry.'

Keira looked him up and down. 'I know you are. I'm sorry for you. But not as much as I am angry. Amy told me that you told her something in confidence, something that was messing you up, but she wouldn't tell me what. She's a good friend like that. Only it makes me feel pretty shitty that you think you can tell her, someone you don't even like – someone you actively hate – that you can tell her something you won't tell me. So what is it Daniel? Please, tell me. What's wrong?'

Daniel looked into her eyes of perfect morning blue, and his lip trembled. *Don't shirk your responsibility to your family.* He couldn't tell her. If he did, he'd lose her forever, in more ways than one. He couldn't tell her that. But there was something he could.

'One minute,' Daniel said, and momentarily disappeared into their bedroom, where he found crumpled in a corner the pair of jeans he'd been wearing on the road, when he first saw his father. Tucked into their pocket, was the printout of the *Herald*.

He returned to the kitchen, and handed it to her. Keira looked at it for a moment, then took it in her hands and read. She blinked at the headline, looked up at Daniel briefly, before scanning the rest of the page. By the time she finished and laid it down on the table, her own lips were trembling.

'Oh Daniel, I'm so sorry.'

Her arms wrapped around him, and Daniel choked back tears of his own as, through her embrace, he looked over her shoulder, and read the contents once more.

HELEN CAWLEY, VICTIM OF FATAL BALLYFARREG MYSTERY CRASH, DIED FROM INJURIES NOT SUSTAINED IN ACCIDENT, AUTOPSY REVEALS.

Mrs. Cawley, victim of the horrific freak car accident that has rocked the community in recent weeks, died not from the collision itself, an autopsy has revealed. The mother of one did not suffer sufficient blunt force trauma, but rather tragically bled out as a result of a miscarriage that saw her lose consciousness. Whether or not the miscarriage was the spark that caused the crash, or indeed if it occurred as a result remains unknown. Her husband, Martin Cawley, (**continue reading page 3**).

Daniel did not keep reading. There was no page three. This was all he had. Not just his mother, but his little brother or sister too, had died because his father had tried to save him. *They don't want to be reasoned with... they can't be. They want what they want, and if they can't get it, they'll take something else.* Daniel couldn't allow them to take Keira and her child.

'Why didn't you tell me?' she whispered in his ear.

And for once, something possessed him to tell the truth. 'Because I'm scared it will happen to you, too.'

Keira's grip on him tightened, as did his on her. 'Well you don't have to worry about that.'

A lump rose in Daniel's throat as he failed to blink away tears. 'All I do is worry about that.'

'Come here,' Keira soothed, and on their last Christmas Eve as a functioning family, Daniel did.

*

Through the steam of a piping hot cup of tea, Daniel watched Rosanna open her presents in front of the fireplace. Keira knelt with her, grinning alongside at each beaming smile a fresh gift of paintbrushes, dolls, and all things Rosanna, produced. She knelt, while Daniel sat.

How was he possibly meant to do this? Less than a week to act, and he had no idea how to proceed. Well, he had *an* idea, but even so much as thinking about it made him physically ill.

New Year's. The party. While everyone was drunk and laughing, he'd have a chance to slip away. Everyone except Keira. He couldn't let her see him leave, that was why he couldn't simply do it beforehand, say, tomorrow. That, and the idea of having to do it at all twisted his stomach anew. She was on edge, constantly. Last night, he'd risen for a piss, and she'd immediately jerked her head from the pillow. *'Where are you going?'*

The party was a chance to put her mind at ease. Surround her with friends, people who made her comfortable. And then snatch her child from under her nose and deliver her to an ancient deity. Daniel rubbed his forehead, and his hand came away slick.

'Okay, just a couple more,' Keira said, and ruffled Rosanna's golden head. 'Dad, do you want to help with the last of the presents while Mum makes herself a coffee?'

'Sure, yeah, sure.'

As Keira drifted off towards the kettle, Daniel slumped to the floor beside Rosanna, whose smile withered slightly at his arrival, for which he was almost glad. If she smiled at him like she had for Keira, he might actually die.

There were four presents left, one for him, one for Keira, one for Rosanna, and, strangely, one left unlabelled. Compulsion drove Daniel's fingers towards this last, the same compulsion that told him not to ask Keira why she hadn't tagged it.

Rosanna watched him gather the gift in his hands, remained expressionless as he lofted it up and down and tried to gauge what was inside from its less than substantial weight.

'Did you wrap this?' he asked softly, but she only stared.

Daniel turned his frown back onto the mystery gift, and noticed for the first time that it was wrapped with twine, not tape or ribbon. Unsure exactly why, he threw a quick glance over his shoulder to make sure Keira was still occupied with the cafetiere, and undid the knot. As the paper crinkled and unfurled beneath him, Daniel's eyes widened.

'Where did you get this?' he whispered.

For her part, Rosanna frowned too. Maybe it wasn't from her.

Deathly pale, with fingers shaking, Daniel ran his hand down the length of the gift. A rope. An old, frayed, tattered rope. Exactly the same as belonged at the gate.

'Do you want a cup?' Keira called, and Daniel scrambled to shove the rope inside his t-shirt, tucked it into his waistband.

'No, no, I'm fine, thanks.'

Rosanna studied him quietly, her orange eyes searing a brand onto his icy heart.

'Jeez, aren't you going to open anything?' Keira asked as she stepped back over. 'Come on Rosanna, what's in your last one?'

Daniel's stomach sank as Keira sat down beside him, cringed at the soft warmth of her hand on his back. In his front, scratching threads tickled his chest.

'Wow, look at that,' Keira marvelled, as Rosanna tore away the last of the wrapping to reveal a brand new sketchpad, A3 size, far larger than anything she already owned. 'Think of all the things you can do with that, isn't that right Dad?'

Daniel swallowed as Rosanna glanced at him once more, then quickly back down to her latest toy, so different from his own. 'Yes,' he mumbled. 'Yes, that's right.'

2

Six days, between Christmas and New Year's, that was what the calendar said. Six days. The calendar, Daniel soon found out, was a liar. Those six bled into one, until there was no "between" at all.

The mirror revealed nothing, it was useless, he'd have been better served fishing out the sketch Rosanna had done up of him, but he stared into it anyways, looking for a sign, a hint, of what was being done to his body. Simply lifting his thumb towards the reflective surface was enough to show it to be an exercise in futility, the grass that had plagued him since that day in the shed did not appear at all, nor did the stems that tickled his nostrils, the mulch beneath his fingernails, the flaky mess that had become of his arms. The mirror was useless, and so was he.

'Daniel, will you bring the drinks in from the car for me please?'

Keira, in the kitchen, getting ready for a party. Keira, with no idea what he meant to do.

Every trace of her, every record, every memory, they'll all be gone by the time the dust has settled.

'Sure,' he called back, and looked into the mirror again, loathed the man that returned his gaze. He had to make sure that dust settled, or they were doomed, all of them. Maybe it wouldn't be so bad. Rosanna did love it there, he'd witnessed it himself, a home away from home. A home, at home, now that he knew what he did. *Life here, it's like no place else. It's open and pure and* free. She would be free, at last, from a father that didn't love her. And a mother who so deeply did.

Daniel let out a long, shuddering breath, wiped his eyes, and went to get the drinks.

Amy was the first to arrive, around eight, and the hug she gave Daniel was clinical at best. She had a bottle of rosé under each arm and a carton of apple juice for Rosanna. Daniel smiled with a mirth he hadn't felt in weeks, and directed her to the bowl on the hallway table where she could leave her car keys so that there'd be no drunken mishaps later on. That was the line, anyways.

'Surprised you've not gone for something harder than that,' he said, eyeing the reddish-pink liquid.

'Aldi's finest,' Amy said. 'And besides, I'm trying to cut back on the so-called "harder" shit. Stomach still hasn't felt quite right since that day you dropped by, though maybe that's got more to do with what was said than what was drank. You talk to Keira yet?'

Slightly taken aback by the upfrontness of it all, Daniel gave a barely perceptible nod. 'Some.'

'Alright, well, go easy on her, yeah? And yourself.'

'Of course,' Daniel said, and managed to resist swallowing until she disappeared into the kitchen where Keira and Rosanna gave a resounding cheer at her arrival.

Joe showed up some time later, fashionably late at half-past the hour, with a sheepish Caitlyn tucked under his arm.

'Well Daniel, long time no see,' Joe said as he clasped Daniel's hand. 'How're you getting on? Better than I left you, I hope. This is Caitlyn, as you may remember.'

189

'Hi,' Daniel said, and winced internally as she stuck out her hand, but she was either too polite or too uncomfortable herself to react to the moisture. 'Glad the two of ye could make it, feel free to stick your keys in the bowl there so A, you don't lose them, and B, I don't have to wrestle them off you later.'

As Joe did so, a little bemused, Daniel peered out past him into the driveway to ensure the road wasn't blocked by either visiting car.

'You've a lovely home,' Caitlyn said, brushing a lock of light brown hair behind her ear as she gave a timid smile.

'Thank you,' Daniel said. 'Have you been in it before?'

Joe coughed, loudly, and quickly changed the subject. 'All in the kitchen, are we?'

'Indeed.'

Keira and Amy rose from the couch once the three stepped inside, and Daniel made manic introductions as the party began in earnest.

'Keira, Caitlyn. Caitlyn, Amy. Amy, Joe. Joe, Keira. Keira, Daniel. Daniel, Keira. Keira, Caitl–'

'Okay we get it,' Keira said, rolling her eyes, and stuck a hand out to Caitlyn. 'Hiya, Daniel has told me literally nothing about you. There's rosé in the fridge, make yourself at home.'

'Thank you so much,' Caitlyn said, and suddenly noticed Rosanna in the armchair. 'Oh, and who's this?'

Joe palmed his forehead. 'Have you no memory woman? Amn't I just after telling you in the car?'

'Ah cut her some slack Joe,' Amy said. 'We can't all have your brilliant mind.'

'Too right,' Joe nodded, and both Daniel and Keira narrowed their eyes at the pair of them. Perhaps that chipping away of Joe's hadn't been as fruitless as they'd thought.

'God, she's awful tall for her age,' Caitlyn was saying. 'Look at you.'

Rosanna giggled with the attention, a knife-twist in Daniel's heart, and he was grateful for Joe's distraction.

'What's the plan of action so,' his oldest friend asked. 'Cans, cans, and, dare I say it, cans?'

Daniel smiled ruefully despite himself and shook his head. 'None for me.'

Joe's mouth dropped open as his face became a perfect imitation of a kicked puppy. 'Why not?'

'Solidarity,' Daniel said, and nodded over at Keira.

'Solid–' Joe began, and caught himself. 'Hang on... you don't mean?'

Keira's smile was shy, Daniel's faked, but Joe's suddenly beamed. 'Jesus Christ! Congratulations, the pair of ye! God I feel old. But congratulations!'

Daniel laughed then, and such was the shock of it that he almost cried. To hide it, he darted over to the fridge. 'What's your poison Joe?' he asked, once he'd cleared his throat. 'Just because I'm not drinking doesn't mean you don't have to.' Quite the opposite, really. If this were going to work, everyone had to be as drunk as humanly possible.

'Jesus, anything. Well, not anything, obviously, none of that IPA crap, but, I mean… Jesus.'

Daniel resurfaced with a bottle of champagne in his hand and a plastered-on grin he both despised and mastered. 'Now who's ready to celebrate?'

Much to his relief, none but Keira declined, though Amy and Joe knocked back their drinks with a ferocity not quite matched by the more nervy Caitlyn.

The night did not wear on, or drag, or toil. It sped, hurtling towards its inevitable conclusion. Daniel kept gazing at Keira out of the corner of his eye, wondered if she was in any way suspicious. Maybe he wanted her to be, maybe he wanted someone – anyone, please, God – to burst through the door and stop him, but of course, no-one did, and of course, she wasn't.

Keira put Rosanna to bed at 9.37pm and Daniel had to excuse himself to the bathroom so that he didn't watch them go. In front of the mirror, he started hyperventilating.

'I can't do this. I can't.'

I tried to save you, and it cost me everything.

Daniel looked at the mirror, and it was his father who stared back. Not his real father, but his father's face, on him. It had to be done. There was nothing else for it. It had to be done.

He stumbled blurry-eyed back into the kitchen to the sound of Kings.

'What's eight?' Caitlyn asked, holding aloft an eight of spades.

'Eight is mate,' Amy was quick to supply. 'Pick someone and anytime you have to drink, so do they.'

'Oh, erm, alright. Daniel.'

Daniel blinked. 'Oh, I'm not –'

'It's fine,' Keira cut across him. 'It's New Year's for God's sake, go ahead.' Before he could protest further, she pressed a whiskey glass into his hand. It looked like someone hadn't forgotten the hard stuff after all.

Daniel stared into the hypnotic golden brown, and wanted nothing more than to swig it down in one go. So he did.

'Alright, that's more fucking like it,' Joe said, clapping his hands as the burn worked its way down Daniel's throat. 'This just became a party. Ten of clubs, what's that?'

'Category,' Amy said. 'Or Never Have I Ever, whichever you pref–'

'Never Have I Ever been thrown out of bed because I couldn't get it up,' Joe said, and looked Daniel dead in the eye.

Daniel pursed his lips as his glass was refilled, temporarily pulled from thoughts of other matters. 'Is that the way it's going to be?'

'Oh, that is most definitely the way it's going to be.'

'Alright,' Daniel said, and took another swig, smaller this time. 'Never Have I Ever –'

'Ah-ah-ah,' Joe interrupted, wagging his finger. 'Not your go, Hot Rod. Keira, I believe you're up.'

Keira squinted. 'Never Have I Ever... gone skinny-dipping?'

'Yes you have,' Amy said, and the two briefly traded glances before Amy shrugged, and drank.

Daniel's nostrils flared, and he tried to dismiss the idea from his mind – God knew it was the least of his concerns – but when the eyes turned to him next, he hadn't quite cooled. 'Never Have I Ever fucked my cousin.'

The phrase "you could hear a pin drop" did not apply. In the aftermath of Daniel's words, the room became the absence of sound. Until Caitlyn snorted.

'I was wondering when that would come up,' she said, and gulped down what was left of her champagne. As the bubbles rose to her head, she shook it clear, and smiled winningly. 'I think I'll need another after that.'

From that point on, it became a night of full-on character assassination.

'Never Have I Ever given head in an alley.'

Keira, with her water, and Amy, with her decidedly not, drank.

'Never Have I Ever refused to go down on a woman because of the smell.'

Joe drank.

'Never Have I Ever thrown up on a partner during a blowjob.'

Caitlyn drank.

'Never Have I Ever relied on my spouse for a living.'

Daniel drank.

'Never Have I Ever tried to fuck a lesbian.'

Keira, Joe, Amy and Daniel all drank, and because Caitlyn felt left out, she did too.

Through it all, Daniel ignored the blurring of his vision, discounted the steady onward march of the clock's hand, but as it neared the eleventh hour, he could do so no longer. On bandied legs, he rose, and, against the will of his heart, plodded towards the hallway.

'Where are you off to?' Keira asked. No-one else had noticed him rise.

'Forgot something in the car,' Daniel said, only lightly slurred.

'My car?' Keira asked. In a private bubble, the conversation existed only in their world.

'Yeah, just a couple extra cans.' He kissed her on the forehead, and she shivered minutely beneath his icy lips. 'I'll be right back.'

'Okay,' Keira said, and that was all. She trusted him. 'Hurry back.'

With that, her eyes returned to the game.

Daniel swallowed, and did not look at the clock as he passed into the hall. He knew what time it was. Three minutes past eleven. Just under an hour, to do his duty.

Gathering three sets of keys from their bowl on the table, he opened the door to Rosanna's room.

1

'Rosanna? Hey, Rosie, wake up.'

Rosanna's nose crinkled, but she did not stir. Daniel could taste the whiskey on his breath as he stooped by her bedside, and shook her gently.

'Earth to Rosanna?'

Orange eyes blinked slowly open. Always orange. Everyone else said they were hazel, but not to Daniel. He'd never seen anything but flame.

'Dad?'

Daniel swallowed the lump in his throat the question caused. 'You have to get up now Rosie, we're going for a trip in the car.'

Rosanna wiped away sleep with little crumpled fists. 'Now?'

'Yes, now. Mum has boring guests in the kitchen so we're going to go have a picnic, down in the forest.'

Rosanna's forehead creased. 'How come we can't have a picnic here?'

Daniel wet his tongue. 'Well, it wouldn't be much of a picnic now would it? Come on, I thought you liked the forest?'

'Used to.'

Daniel resisted the urge to glance over his shoulder. Laughter emanated from the other room, he still had some time. 'What do you mean, "used to"?'

Rosanna's face became a pout.

'Is it… is it because of the dream you had?'

She was silent for a moment, then nodded.

'What happens in the dream, Rosie?'

Her lower lip trembled, and she let out a rattling breath. 'You… push me.'

Daniel swallowed. Despite the warmth of the room and the heat of the drink, his skin prickled. 'I *push* you?'

Rosanna nodded.

'Rosie, I would never push you.' The words were out before he could even think about them, and what was worse, they were true. He believed they were true.

'Okay,' Rosanna said at last, after an eternally tense moment of silence. 'Can I bring my blanket?'

'Sure thing, we just have to be quiet going out, okay? We don't want to disturb Mum's boring guests.'

'Okay.'

Daniel held his breath as Rosanna slipped out from the bed and draped the blanket around her shoulders. For all the fuss Caitlyn and Mary before her had made about her being so big for her age, Daniel didn't see it at all. She was so terribly small.

'Can we –'

'Shhh!' he hissed as he opened the door to the hallway. Sounds of laughter increased. No-one had heard. No-one would even notice he was gone, not until they were far, far away.

'Okay, follow me.'

Cold wind buffeted the pair as Daniel's ears became attuned to the crunch of every piece of gravel beneath his steps. Even with the front door closed he was certain that those in the kitchen would be able to hear such earth-shattering, heart-wrenching claps of thunder.

Keira's car was a warm relief, but he saw the sweat that licked his palms increase tenfold as he fiddled with Rosanna's seatbelt, before eventually getting round to his own. A glance at the door, hallway cloaked in darkness, Daniel took a deep breath. He turned the key in the ignition.

In the same moment, the hallway light flicked on.

'Fuck!'

Reverse, forward, clutch, fuck, go, GO!

'Dad!'

A silhouette appeared in the window, and a stunned Keira stepped out onto the gravel. In the short slice of time, before her car shot out onto the road and tore away from sight, potentially for good, she saw it all. Daniel, in the driver's seat, sweating and frantic. Rosanna, just beside, still in her pyjamas and draped in a blanket, wrapped deep inside and rocking. Keira screamed.

Daniel almost crushed the steering wheel beneath the force of his grip as she dwindled to a speck in the rear-view mirror, the road ahead unfurling in various shrouded twists and turns, pushing his drunken, petrified state to its very limits, while Rosanna watched on with mouth agape as Keira's fading tortured wail rent his soul in two.

'Why is Mum shouting?' Rosanna asked, looking desperately over her shoulder. 'Why isn't she with her guests? Doesn't she know we're going for a picnic? Didn't you tell her?'

The questions came faster than he could answer, faster than he could register. 'Because we were being too loud,' he managed at last.

'She looked scared.'

'She was just upset.'

Fields blurred, road unravelled, the gate revealed itself to them, open. Of course it was open, Daniel had the rope, didn't he? He almost laughed. Almost.

'You're not going to push me, are you?' Rosanna asked as the car wheeled off new-laid tarmac onto timeless stone.

'No,' Daniel said, as the forest unveiled itself around them. 'I'm not going to push you. We're just going for a picnic, remember?'

Rosanna wrung her shaking hands, glanced over her shoulder into the back seat. 'Where's the food?'

Daniel gulped. Tree after tree after tree fell away behind them, each one no different from the last. 'It's in the boot,' he croaked.

11.13pm. Forty-seven minutes. It was all going to be okay, if he could just get through those next forty-seven minutes. It was all –

Keira's car lurched forward, chugged once, and unceremoniously died.

'No,' Daniel whispered. He thumped the wheel, and the horn gave a sharp *toot* in reply, making both he and Rosanna leap. He turned to her. 'Come on.'

'Where are we going?'

Daniel pointed forward, the way ahead lit by Keira's headlights. 'Just through the trees at the end there, there's a little spot where we can go.'

'Why can't we just have the picnic here?'

'Because,' Daniel said, as he fiddled with her belt once more. 'We can't see the stars from here. Don't you want to see the stars?'

Rosanna didn't answer and for this Daniel was grateful. He so desperately wished that they were here for nothing more than that, that they could simply look at the stars together, out here, together. He swallowed the mental image alongside his bile.

'What about the food?' Rosanna asked, as he began pushing her along down the road.

'It's there already,' Daniel said, constantly checking back the way they'd come.

'I thought you said –'

'I said it's there already!'

Rosanna's lip quivered and Daniel's heart died.

'Come on Rosie, it's not that much further, we're almost…' Daniel stopped. His voice was too loud. Far, far too loud. It was the only sound at all. How could that be? Even at its most isolated, there could always be heard the faint rustling of branches, the kiss of wind on the –

Trees. But there weren't any trees. No trees at all. Movement became an impossibility, as he saw what had replaced them.

All around, in parallel straits that lined either side of the road, were people. People no human should ever wish to see, and yet people these had been. Reanimated beyond death, the dozens of crippled, warped, agonised faces that stared back at Daniel made Martin Cawley look handsome. Flesh had been rendered non-existent beneath layers of stretching bark, limbs a forgotten, hopeless endeavour, faces an irreconcilable wreck, but, as always, worst of all were the eyes. Through a mask of wood and vegetation, the eyes remained, weathered, beaten, and utterly lost. Lost, but not soulless. Soulless would have been an improvement. Each stared back at Daniel with fountains of unutterable pain, and begged him for their end.

'Rosanna,' he whispered, still unmoving. 'Do you see –'

'*Daniel!*'

Daniel's head whipped round as tendrils of dread trickled down his spine, but there was no sight to match the voice. Another sounded.

'*Rosanna!*'

The first had been Amy, only after this second could he tell that. The latter was Keira.

'Go,' Daniel said.

'But –'

'I said GO!'

Frozen no longer, the pair raced on towards the road's end, where the forest took up again proper, and though Daniel knew there was no time to waste, especially now, he couldn't help but slow as they passed one "tree" in particular.

'Dad?'

Martin Cawley peered back at Daniel with glazed eyes, but no recognition flickered beneath that cracked and rotting surface.

'Dad?' Daniel asked again, slowing just enough that he could hear a faint reply.

Through broken lips, it rattled softly, 'Who are –'

But the rest was lost to the forest as he and Rosanna both disappeared beyond the road, and into the trees again. Real trees.

Just in front of him Rosanna tripped on an upturned root and Daniel caught her before she could fall. Big, terrified eyes stared back at him in the moment before he hoisted her onto his chest, yet despite it all her tiny fingers clung to him with a desperation that caused him to claw back tears.

Rosanna's voice was a whisper. 'Why is Mum shouting at us?'

'Because she doesn't understand what's happening.'

'Oh,' she breathed. 'Do you?'

Daniel didn't answer. He'd noticed something ahead. A light, sort of. No, a haze. Green, a green haze. Fog, but like none he'd ever seen. He almost laughed, again. There was a book to be written on things he hadn't seen. The further they walked, the thicker it grew, until the way forward became an emerald mist around them.

'*Daniel!*'

A man's voice. Joe had come, too. They'd all come, of course. Who wouldn't?

There was no going back. Onwards through the green he plunged, the only way to end it all to make sure it never happened in the first place.

He heard crying, and was about to tell Rosanna it would be okay, everything soon, finally, would be okay. Then he realised the sobs were his own.

The trees thinned until there were none at all, and the carpet of leaves that had paved their way underfoot became grass. They'd reached the clearing, but the fog did not lift.

'Do you see a tree, Rosanna?' his voice was barely recognisable, even to himself.

'*Daniel!*'

'*Rosanna!*'

Whatever the child had been about to say died on her lips, but it didn't matter, Daniel saw what lay in front. A tree, yes, but not the one from his dreams, of course not the one from his dreams, such a monstrosity couldn't exist in reality, a simple tree, a regular tree. Where it stood was anything but.

A raised embankment, some two metres high, rose up from the earth, and spread around in a perfect circle, another eight metres wide, and it was here, atop its centre, where sprung the tree, a guiding lighthouse in the fog, a standing sentinel, in the middle of a faery fort.

'We have to climb it,' Daniel said, remembering his dream. That was where they'd be waiting, at its summit, hidden betwixt leaf and branches. Unseen.

'Why?' Rosanna asked.

'We just do,' he said, as he hoisted her up onto the embankment, and scrambled up in turn. Behind them, the voices were getting closer.

'*Rosanna, are you there?*'

'*Daniel?*'

Daniel's skin tingled as he rose to his feet, stood on hallowed ground, but he did not allow himself to give it thought as he raced to the tree's base, and held out his hand for Rosanna.

'Come on!'

Rosanna looked at him, then up at the tree. It's top was shrouded in fog. 'You're not going to push me, are you?'

Daniel stared back, into those glowing orange eyes, and swallowed. 'No. I'm not going to push you.'

'Do you promise?'

'I promise.'

'Do you love me?'

Daniel's mouth fell open, as what was left of his heart crumbled away entirely. Rosanna only watched him, saw him, and as he finally saw her too, he whispered, 'Yes, Rosie. Yes, I love you.'

She took his hand, and Daniel lifted her up, utterly weightless, to the first nook in the bark, nudged her gently on her way until she was climbing herself. She knew how, of course. She was a natural.

Daniel chewed back his sobs as he followed suit, blotted his ears from the screaming voices that seemed to be coming from all around now.

'*Daniel?*'

'*Rosanna?*'

Fists battered branches and fingers tugged at leaves that blocked his way, but further on, Rosanna was able to weave in and out of the obstacles with ease.

'*Is that…*'

'*Oh my God.*'

They'd found them.

Daniel's measured ascent became frantic, seeking handholds where there were none, pulling himself forward by sheer strength of will alone as the green fog continued to thicken.

'Daniel!' Keira shrieked. 'Daniel, what are you doing?'

Similar cries erupted from below, but as Daniel clawed further forward still, they were overrode by a new voice, which came from deep within the centre of his brain.

'Welcome, Daniel of the Cawley clan. Have you come to make good the promises of your name-sake?'

The smooth lyricism of the hypnotic words stuck him in place. Just ahead, Rosanna had noticed he'd stopped, and turned back to look at him, though he could barely see her through the fog.

'What promises?' he asked, but before the voice could answer, he plucked one forth himself from the recesses of his mind. A deal. His father had mentioned a deal.

'That each male heir must conceive a child in our sanctum, and that it be returned to us when the time comes, so that you may know what it is like to watch something you love disappear before your eyes.'

Tears flowed ceaselessly down Daniel's cheeks as the screams below became one big wail of protest. 'I didn't know I loved her. I didn't know.'

'This should be easy for you then. Give her to us.'

Daniel shook his head. 'Please, no. Please. There has to be some other –'

'Give, or we will take.'

Daniel swallowed, as Keira shrieked a fresh, wordless cry below. Rosanna was totally consumed by the fog now, but for her faint outline. Maybe that would make it easier, that he didn't have to look.

'How?' Daniel croaked. Dimly, he was aware that there was something in his hands besides bark and leaves.

'Push her.'

His soul left him. 'I can't.'

Rosanna stood just ahead, just in reach, delicately poised on the surface of a branch.

Below, they were all roaring now.

'Don't do this Daniel,' Joe's petrified plea.

'Stop! Jesus Christ, stop!' Caitlyn's terrified roar.

'It's not real Daniel,' Amy cried. 'For the love of God, Daniel, it's not real!'

Through all the crying, Keira's won out, a simple, gut-wrenching screech of pure, maternal horror, 'Daniel, *please*!'

Daniel could not allow himself to listen, could not allow himself to falter. Whatever they said, whatever they saw, it *was* real, and it would all soon become undone.

'*Push her, Daniel.*'

He had to make it count.

'*Give her to us.*'

He had to ensure that the dust settled.

'*PUSH HER!*'

He had to do his duty.

His pulsing hands shook with illness and fear as he laid them upon his only daughter's back.

'Dad?'

The fog lifted, and he pushed.

In the second before she fell, Daniel saw it all. Saw where he was sitting, in a tree branch three metres from the ground. Saw the distraught faces of those who stood below, begging in slow-motion to prevent an action that could not be undone. Saw Rosanna in front of him, as his hands left her back.

Rosanna, with a rope around her neck. The rope from the famine gate. The rope that had been given to Daniel.

Rosanna falling.

In the next second, before the rope would tauten and surely snap her neck, Daniel whipped his head round, his face a portrait of wild-eyed terror, and saw at last, for the very first time, the instigator who'd set all these events to motion. A faery.

Older than time and slyer than death, through eyes of utmost black on a moon-slick face, it looked back at Daniel, and reeked of earth, moss, and deceit. Then it grinned.

The faery winked at him, and was gone.

Printed in Great Britain
by Amazon

20898666R00123